SIERRA SUMMIT

by VIRGINIA BESAW EVANSEN

Decorations by ALLAN THOMAS

This is the tale of the first successful crossing of the Western mountains to California by wagons. The Stephens-Murphy-Townsend party started from Missouri in March, 1844—twenty-six men, eight women and seventeen children—headed for the Sierra Nevada Mountains.

Their adventures are told from the viewpoint of Moses Schallenberger, who started off feeling it was rather a lark, and, with his friend, became involved in foolishness. Dust and thirst, the wear of the trail, the fear of Indians, the agonizing difficulties of moving the wagons up and over and down the mountains, of bringing them across water, the responsibility of securing food from the country, turn the seventeen-year-old into a man.

Moses' brother-in-law, Dr. Townsend, and the others carry valuable cargo. Moses stays behind to guard the wagons when the others must leave them to save their lives. Since the issue remains in doubt until the end, this true story makes exciting reading, bringing alive the drama on Donner Pass and in early California history.

SIERRA

SUMMIT

SIERRA SUMMIT

by

VIRGINIA BESAW EVANSEN

Decorations by ALLAN THOMAS

DAVID McKAY COMPANY, INC.
New York
1967

Sierra Summit

COPYRIGHT © 1967 BY

Virginia Besaw Evansen

29043

LIBRARY OF CONGRESS CATALOG CARD NUMBER: 67–15045

MANUFACTURED IN THE UNITED STATES OF AMERICA

To
Kenny

⤙ FOREWORD ⤚

THE STORY of the Stephens-Murphy-Townsend party is usually given only a line or two, or a short paragraph, in histories of the emigration to California. Since this group of twenty-six men, eight women, and seventeen children that started for California in March, 1844, and arrived there in December, 1844, brought the first wagons over the Sierra Nevada and pioneered the route through the Donner Pass, which was later followed by so many wagon trains, it would seem they deserve more mention than this.

Because this party arrived safely, John Sutter could send Caleb Greenwood to Fort Hall in 1845 to urge the emigrants to take the California trail, assuring them that wagons could pass through the mountains.

Perhaps this party has been ignored because so few records were kept by them, and because the tragic deaths of almost half of the Donner party were more dramatic than the story of the Stephens party that survived the journey.

This is the story of Moses Schallenberger, a seventeen-year-old member of the party. All of the characters in the story were real people, and, as far as I can discover, the events described actually occurred. The thoughts and conversation of the characters are, of course, fictionalized, but they could have been the thoughts and speech of these people who traveled the Oregon Trail to Fort Hall and then pioneered the trail into California.

Historians who do mention this party differ as to dates, the number of wagons, and the number of people in the company. I have used twelve wagons because I find it reasonable to believe that both Caleb Greenwood and Joseph Foster had wagons. Greenwood was a devoted father who would not have left his small children in Missouri, and he couldn't have taken them through on horseback. Since his two young daughters were enrolled in school in California in 1846, it seems probable that they came with the party in 1844. There was no reason for Joseph Foster to have remained in the mountains unless he had a wagon to guard. However, the exact number of wagons is immaterial. What is important is that these wagons were the first to cross the mountains into California.

To avoid confusion, I have used the present name of the Humboldt River. In 1844 it was known as Mary's River.

Colin Lucas and the staff of the Sunnyvale Public

Library have given me much valuable assistance in my research. I am deeply indebted to Olive Rambo Cook. Her help and encouragement made this book possible.

Virginia Besaw Evansen

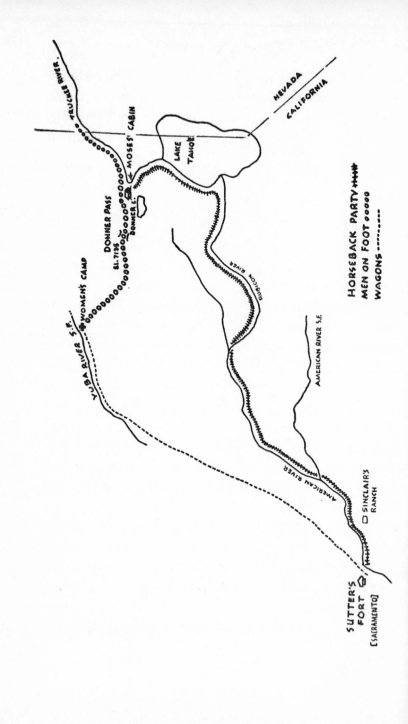

✤ 1 ✤

MOSES SCHALLENBERGER stirred uneasily in the saddle as he waited for the wagons to catch up with him. He was so impatient—so tired of the slow pace set by the plodding oxen that he felt ready to explode.

He smiled at his sister Elizabeth, who sat on the hard seat of the first wagon, and waved to Allen Montgomery trudging beside the oxen pulling the second wagon. He knew he should ride back and help Dr. John drive the extra cattle, but he leaned forward, patted his sleek brown mare on the shoulder, and touched her flank lightly with his heel. "Come on, girl," he said. "Let's go."

He passed the two covered wagons lurching slowly along the muddy, rutted road, and cantered up the hill. They were almost at the meeting place—Nisnabotna—and he just couldn't wait another moment. He had to see for himself.

At the top of the gentle rise he peered anxiously

1

ahead, then wheeled his horse and galloped back to the wagons.

"Elizabeth!" he shouted. "There are hundreds of wagons, and horses, and cattle! Hundreds of them—all going west!"

Elizabeth smiled—a broad smile of relief. "That means we can really get started," she said.

"Get started! What do you think we did two weeks ago?" Allen yelled. "I'd say we started west then."

Moses grinned at his limping, mud-spattered friend. "I guess we really started two years ago when we began planning the journey," he said. Suddenly he realized how lucky he was. He wouldn't have to walk most of the way from Missouri to California as Allen, who had no one to drive his teams, would. Trudging alongside the plodding oxen that pulled the wagons at two miles an hour on a good road would be a chore. Right now they moved at less than a snail's pace through the slippery clay ruts that passed for roads at this time of year. Moses was fortunate to have a good horse, and he would have plenty of time to hunt. He had dreamed all winter about the buffalo of the Platte Valley. He was going to shoot the first one he saw, or bust an arm trying!

If only some of the wagons at Nisnabotna were on their way to California! They had planned this trip so long, and he was both worried and impatient. They simply had to go this year! Elizabeth was frail, and he knew that Dr. John didn't want her to spend another winter in Missouri where malaria with its chills and fever crept relentlessly across the land, killing settler after settler.

Dr. John had first talked of emigrating when he heard of Anton Robidoux's speeches praising California. The trader claimed there was fertile land, wild horses and cattle, vast valleys, soft winds, sunshine all year, friendly Indians, and no malaria.

They had planned carefully and worked hard for months. They bent hickory staves over the farm wagon and spread canvas across the top for a cover. They sold the farm and their furniture and bought oxen, corn meal, side pork, and salt to carry with them. Last fall Elizabeth had dried twice the amount of fruit she usually did, so there would be plenty for the journey, and Dr. John had laid in an extra supply of drugs.

Then Dr. John heard about Joe Chiles. He had left Missouri in 1843 with a wagonload of goods to sell in California. This was Chiles' second trip west. He had been a member of the Bidwell-Bartleson party in 1841. Although that party had lost its wagons, Joe Chiles maintained he would get his through safely this time.

No one knew whether Chiles had succeeded, but Dr. John figured the idea was a shrewd one, and decided the Townsends weren't going to be paupers in the new land. So they had traveled to St. Louis two months ago and purchased bolts of broadcloth and silk and satin—light goods that wouldn't overload the wagon—luxuries that the Californians would find difficult to resist. Dr. John declared he would build a great house for Elizabeth with the profit.

John Townsend was a good husband for Elizabeth, Moses thought gratefully, and a good doctor, and just as kind to him as if he were his father. Dr. John was hearty and openhanded, but sometimes Moses wished he wouldn't lecture him quite so often—always telling him that it was time he grew up, that he was old enough to consider the consequences of his deeds, and that he shouldn't act so impetuously.

Moses could barely remember his father and mother. He had been only six when they died eleven years ago. Since then he had lived with Elizabeth and Dr. John. As he looked back at his sister, his blood chilled as if he had caught the malaria that filled this land of Missouri. That was why he had worked so hard and willingly when Dr. John decided to emigrate. Dr. John said they were going to a golden land where no one was sick, where there were miles of rich land to graze cattle and men grew wealthy selling hides.

When their neighbor, Allen Montgomery, decided to join them, Dr. John announced they would start this spring, even though the two wagons might have to travel alone.

Allen had worked with them during the winter. He had made extra shoes for the oxen, and reinforced the ironwork on the wagons. During the long winter, he had found time to make a pair of pistols for Moses, the first guns the boy had ever owned.

It had been a wet spring, with the rain falling as though the sky were a vast pump. Finally the roads had dried out enough for the oxen to slog through the ruts, and two weeks ago they had started for Nisnabotna where, Dr. John had heard, a company of west-bound emigrants was gathering.

Moses had been apprehensive for several days, wondering what they would do if no one else was going west. Now that he had seen the wagons, he felt as if a great weight had rolled off his shoulders. He whistled a tune and proudly touched the belt buckled snugly around his waist. The pistols gleamed at his hips. They made him feel like a man, and he sat erect in the saddle as the small company's wagons rolled slowly up the slope.

Elizabeth laughed at Moses as the wagons crested the top of the hill. "If that isn't just like you!" she said. "Always exaggerating. Hundreds of wagons indeed! I don't believe there's half that many."

"Well, maybe not a hundred." Moses grinned at his sister. "But there are lots of wagons. Enough so that we'll be safe."

Nisnabotna was a hive of activity that afternoon of March 1, 1844. Oxen bawling, horses and cattle munching tender shoots of green prairie grass, small children racing around the wagons in never-ending games of tag, women starting suppers in black iron pots suspended over open fires or on the tops of small cook stoves, men inspecting the wagons to see how wheels and axles had fared during the initial weeks of travel.

Dr. John led his oxen to a spreading oak tree near the edge of the encampment, and maneuvered the wagon so there would be shade for Elizabeth. He directed his hired man, Francis Deland, to take the horses and cattle out to graze.

Moses glanced at the nearby wagons, then unsaddled his brown mare, rubbed her down, and led her to a small stream to drink. His heart pounded with excitement as he thought of the long journey ahead—the hundreds of miles between Nisnabotna and the mountains. He tethered his horse and hurried back to the wagon where Dr. John was starting to pitch the tent that he and Elizabeth slept in.

"Let's find out right away how many of these people are going to California," Moses suggested eagerly.

Dr. John pursed his lips. "You're in an all-fired hurry, Moses. But I guess it would do no harm to walk around the camp while Elizabeth prepares supper. The sooner we find out how many of these people are heading for California, the sooner we'll get a company organized."

Allen Montgomery limped toward them. "I'm not sure I can walk another ten steps, but I'm coming, too.

I hope someone is going our way. I get a shaky feeling thinking about traveling alone." He stumbled and kicked a rock out of his path. "The soles of these boots should be three times as thick. My blisters are *growing* blisters."

Dr. John glanced around the bustling camp and then walked toward the nearest wagon. "What's your destination?" he hailed a man chopping wood for his fire.

"Oregon."

"Do you know of anyone heading for California?"

"You crazy, too?" The man lowered his axe and stared at Dr. John.

Dr. John jumped at the last word. "Then you've heard of someone going to California?"

"There's a whole passel of folks over by the river about seven wagons down. An old fellow named Murphy is boss of the bunch. It's an entire family. Married children and their children. Murphy says he's taking them all to California. I say he's loony. Wagons can't make it over the great mountains."

"Murphy, eh? We'll find them." Dr. John started toward the river. "Come on, Moses." He turned impatiently to the boy. "What are you staring at?"

Moses was watching a wagon lurch down the rutted road. "Did you ever see anyone who looked like that before?" he asked.

A long-haired, scraggly-bearded man with a nose as hooked as a turkey's beak stopped his oxen beside them. He had a long, cavernous face atop a scrawny, stretched-out neck. Moses decided he was uglier than a chicken hawk.

"The name is Stephens," the man said, walking up to Dr. John and holding out his hand. "Elisha Stephens. Heard it said that some folks were heading for California. Decided I would mosy west, too."

"Glad to meet you." Dr. John shook his hand. "I'm Dr. John Townsend. This is Moses Schallenberger and Allen Montgomery. California's our destination." He pushed his hat back, openly inspecting Stephens and his wagon. "I've just discovered there's a party of Murphys here with the same idea," he continued, apparently satisfied with his study of the man. "We're going over to talk with them now. Care to join us?"

Elisha Stephens nodded, and they resumed their walk toward the river. Moses lagged behind, looking at the wagons and people, noticing a trim girl whose hair shone coppery red as she bent over her fire. She smiled as he walked past her, and Moses smiled back.

He hurried to catch up with Dr. John who had stopped beside a closely clustered group of wagons from which children were tumbling like puppies. Dr. John glanced at the seven wagons briefly, then walked briskly up to an older man who was obviously in charge.

"Is your name Murphy?"

"That's right. Martin Murphy."

"I understand you're heading for California."

"That's right, too. My whole family. We're leaving for the Bluffs as soon as the roads dry out."

"Are any of the other people gathered here planning to go to California?"

Martin Murphy, a well-muscled, stalwart man whom Moses judged to be much older than Dr. John, maybe even fifty or sixty, because of his graying hair and the patient sadness of his eyes, shook his head. "Just our seven wagons. The rest are going to Oregon."

"Allen Montgomery and I have wagons and good oxen," Dr. John announced. "I'm Dr. John Townsend, a medical doctor," he continued somewhat pompously. He paused for a moment, appraising first Martin Murphy and then the wagons. "Your equipment appears to be good, as if you had planned for a hard journey." He hesitated, then gestured at the scrawny man standing beside him. "This man is named Stephens. He says he's going to California, too."

"Aiming there," Elisha Stephens said. "I figured there would be folks heading that way this spring so I threw my gear and traps in the wagon." Elisha Stephens clipped off his words as if he found talking distasteful. He glanced around at the encampment and then turned back to Martin Murphy. "Seen anything of an old man, name of Greenwood? He looks like an Injun. Heard he left St. Louis for the west. Caleb Greenwood's journeyed over the plains and into the high mountains. He's a trapper. Wife was a Crow. He can palaver with the Injuns. I planned to tie up with him."

"Not yet, but more wagons arrive every day. It seems as if most of Missouri's planning to go west this spring," Martin Murphy answered. "I can't blame them either," he said bitterly. "This land's filled with sickness and death."

He turned to Moses. "My son John is over by the bank fishing. He's about your age. Why don't you go down and get acquainted with him while we make some plans?"

By noon the next day Nisnabotna looked as if Mr. Murphy was right in saying all of Missouri was moving west. Moses walked around the camp, counting the wagons. Forty of them. All common farm wagons like their own, converted for the journey with hickory staves bent over the tops. Some were covered with coarse osnaburg, some with heavier canvas, and all of them had oval openings at the front and back for ventilation.

Most of the families had tents, too, pitched beside the wagons. Horses, cows, and oxen were herded by the men and older boys. The young girls helped their mothers and watched the small children.

As Moses counted the wagons, he hoped that some of the emigrants would change their minds and go to

California. It seemed to him that with a larger company there would be a better chance of getting through safely.

All of the men in the camp drifted toward the center of the wagons at noon. Moses stayed close to Dr. John's heels. He saw Martin Murphy in the middle of a group listening to Elisha Stephens who stood beside a tall, brawny, bearded man. The stranger had red-rimmed eyes that he blinked continually, and he wore filthy, ancient buckskins. He was the leatheriest, leanest, dirtiest man Moses had ever seen. Standing beside him were two tall boys in fringed buckskins who appeared to be copies of the old man. Moses realized this must be Caleb Greenwood, the trapper who had been all the way to the South Pass and beyond! With increasing excitement, Moses followed Dr. John through the crowd so that he could hear what was being planned.

"Sure I know the way," Mr. Greenwood was saying. "So does old Hitchcock there. He's been a mountain man, and a good one." He pointed to another grizzled, buckskin-clad, older man standing at the back of the group. "I went with Manuel Lisa and Ashley when the trappers was kings of the mountains," he continued, throwing out his chest. "Been over the back of the mountains and beyond. To California, too."

"Then you can guide us to California?" Mr. Murphy asked.

"Ain't sure about that now. I was there once years

ago, over a pass no wagon could stand. I can take you through the South Pass to Fort Hall. Trail's plain as the skin on your face. The trappers took plenty horses and wagons far as Fort Hall. My sons and I can find campsites and water for you." Caleb Greenwood shifted his rifle and pulled at his long beard. "We ain't planning on California. I'm hankering to spend my days on the Yellowstone."

"We're going to California," Mr. Murphy said. "Mr. Hitchcock has already joined our company, but doubts his ability to guide us. There are eleven wagons now, with ample supplies and oxen, and even a real doctor— Townsend, here."

The trapper scratched his greasy head. "You ain't going to get them wagons through. Them California mountains are like stone walls stretched clear to the sky. The snow in winter is so deep neither men nor wagons can move. The cold would freeze the heart out of a man. Why don't you go to Oregon?"

"These wagons are going to California." Martin Murphy's voice was flat and harsh. He sounded as if he would pull them by himself if necessary. "We're leaving as soon as it stops raining, and we'll be over the mountains before winter. We need a guide. Can you do it?"

Mr. Greenwood pulled at his beard again. "Guide you through the pass to Fort Hall? Sure. That's plumb easy. But California— Well, now." He scuffed a moccasin in the dirt, glanced appraisingly at the wagons, and then studied his sons for a long moment.

Moses caught his breath and waited, letting it out in sudden relief as the trapper turned and said to Martin Murphy, "Maybe I ain't all that set on going to the Yellowstone after all." He hesitated only a moment. "Yep, I'll do it!"

During the weeks that went by before the roads dried out enough to be passable, Dr. John and Martin Murphy talked, begged, and cajoled the owners of the other wagons into joining their company. Finally they all agreed to journey together as far as Fort Hall, and some of the more adventurous Oregon-bound travelers even thought they might try the dangerous trail to California since the company would have an experienced guide.

Moses herded cattle, carried water and firewood for Elizabeth, and dreamed of buffalo while waiting impatiently for the rain to stop. Dr. John and Martin Murphy worried about the long delay, but Mr. Greenwood explained that the grass wouldn't be high enough to feed the cattle for another month; that it was an unusually cold, wet spring.

It was not until early May that the company could leave for Council Bluffs. Moses brought his brown mare alongside the wagon and looked ahead and behind as the captain shouted the order for the wagons to move. He rode proudly and held his head high as befitted a corporal of the guard. After Caleb Greenwood had agreed to guide the party to Fort Hall, they had held an election. All of the men voted for a captain, and to Moses' surprise, they had chosen the ugly, bird-nosed Elisha Stephens. He thought it was strange that a man who had been a blacksmith and hunter had been chosen captain over Dr. John Townsend who had books in his wagon and had graduated from Lexington Medical College, and over the Murphys who were educated people, too. But maybe the men knew what they were doing. Captain Stephens had organized the train promptly and had made both Moses and John Murphy corporals of the guard.

The Greenwoods were a queer bunch, Moses decided. Mr. Greenwood's rheumy eyes, scraggly gray hair, and ancient buckskins made him look like an old chief who belonged in a council tent, but he strode firmly, with his head erect. His grown sons obeyed their father instantly, but Moses noticed that he was indulgent with his little girls—especially with the younger, Sarah Mojave.

John Greenwood's young Indian wife mothered the two girls, but kept away from the other women, fleeing to the wagon like a shy bird when they tried to talk with her.

Moses glanced back at the wagon just behind Allen's where a smiling girl, her red hair almost hidden by a slat sunbonnet, rode on the seat. She waved to him, and he waved back, an exuberant salute, then turned to watch the road.

The wagons rolled ahead in a long line with the cattle and extra horses herded at one side. Captain Stephens had explained the order of the march. The lead wagon one day would go to the end of the line the next day, and each wagon would move up so that all would have an equal chance at the open trail. No one would have too much dust that way. Moses wondered why the captain had talked about dust as he watched the wagons lurch in the slippery clay ruts. At this rate they would spend years on the trail, struggling toward California!

It took two weeks to reach Council Bluffs. The company settled into the routine of an early rising, a rest at noon to eat and let the cattle graze, and the welcome halt when the sun slid toward the western horizon. Captain Stephens ordered the wagons into a circle each night, with the cattle inside. Dr. John protested that there were no hostile Indians on this side of the river. He claimed that these foolish precautions wasted time and made the company miserable.

Captain Stephens explained that they had better learn how to live on the trail before they met the Indians. Since the territory of the thieving Otoes was just across the Missouri River, they would have trouble and risk losing cattle if they weren't prepared. The captain added tersely that the company would obey him as long as he was in charge.

When they reached Council Bluffs, the water was high and the owner of the ferry, a little flatboat, refused to take them across the Missouri River until the water subsided. Captain Stephens said they could make good use of the time by checking and repairing wagons and gear. Moses helped Allen inspect their wagons. The wheels were strong and wide, and the iron tires were tight. The axles had survived the jolting in the deep ruts without damage. Moses started to saddle his horse.

Elizabeth stopped him as he adjusted the stirrups. "It seems as if you have nothing much to do, Moses. I want to wash clothes. You can help Francis carry water."

"Golly-whillikers, Sis," he protested, "John Murphy and I were going to explore."

"You'll have plenty of miles to explore," Elizabeth said sharply. "All the way from here to California. Right now I need water."

Moses brought one bucket from the river and held it out for Elizabeth to inspect.

"Can't you find a small stream with cleaner water?" she asked. "The clothes will be dirtier than they are now if I wash them in this stuff. It's too thick to drink and too thin to chew."

Moses shrugged. "Even the creeks are high from all

the rain we've had, and you can see what the river is like."

The Missouri was high with melted snow from its mountain tributaries and filled with yellow mud that made huge circles as it swirled by the bluffs. We would drown if we tried to ford it, Moses thought. He shivered as he studied the river, wondering if the small flatboat could make it across safely.

As they waited, Moses grew restless. It seemed that the spring rains would never stop, that the river would never go down. Moses heard Captain Stephens talking with Dr. John and Martin Murphy and realized that the men were anxious about the delay, fearing that they would have to push the oxen too fast once they were on the trail.

Finally, on the eighteenth of May, Moses watched their wagon being loaded onto the boat. He held his breath for a moment, afraid that the small boat would sink under the weight, but it stayed afloat. He watched intently as the men rowed the ferry across the wide, muddy river, angling downstream to take advantage of the current.

At noon Captain Stephens decided it was time to get the cattle across and told the men to bring the herd down to the bank. Moses mounted his horse and helped with the drive.

The first cattle balked on the edge of the swift water. "They won't go!" Moses shouted. Captain Stephens pushed through the herd and laid his whip on the backs of the leaders, forcing them into the water.

"Move, you critters!" he shouted. Then he turned and called to Martin and John Murphy, "Come on. Give us a hand!"

The animals moved reluctantly, bellowing as they were shoved into the river by the pressure of those behind them and the sting of the whips. The current caught the cattle. They bawled in terror and rolled their eyes as they were swept downstream. The leaders turned in a circle toward the shore, and the cattle behind them climbed on their backs, frantic to get out of the water. They drifted about a hundred yards downstream and floundered out on the muddy bank.

"Stop them!" Captain Stephens yelled, barely able to make himself heard above the bawling of the cattle and the screams of the watching women. Moses, who was helping to hold the rest of the herd back, swallowed hard as he watched the cattle fighting the current, trying desperately to reach a secure footing. The oxen sank into the mud and sand, first hoof-deep, then to their knees.

"They're stuck!" Moses shouted to John Murphy. John and his father wheeled their horses and started down the bank to the oxen that bellowed louder as they sank deeper into the mud. The Murphys roped the nearest one, jerked him out, and threw a rope around the next one. Moses swung his horse around and rode down the bank to help.

"I can't pull this one loose," John yelled. "Give me a hand with the rope." Moses added his weight to John's, straining as hard as he could. The ox came out of the mud with a sucking sound.

"It must be quicksand!" Moses started to shout, then mumbled the dread word. He threw his rope around the neck of the next ox, already deeper in the mud than the first one. Dr. John and Martin Murphy added their weight, but they could not free the animal.

"He's stuck fast. He's too big to pull out!" John shouted.

"Pull harder, boys," Martin Murphy ordered. "Get some picks and shovels! We need the oxen. Every last one of them!"

Four more of the frightened cattle lumbered out on the bank, one of them climbing over the back of the ox Moses had roped, pushing him deeper into the mud. Dr. John, Martin Murphy, and Allen Montgomery grabbed shovels and started digging the cattle out.

"I'll get more help. Hang on!" Martin Murphy shouted to Moses as he realized that digging wouldn't free the mired animals.

"He's pulling us down." Moses tightened his rope, but his horse slid several more feet as the ox pulled them closer to the edge of the water. "What'll I do?" he yelled.

"Loose your rope. Let go now!" Captain Stephens ordered.

Moses obeyed instantly, panting for breath, as the ox settled deeper into the mud. He watched hopelessly for a moment, sick with horror. Then he shut his eyes and clapped his hands over his ears to shut out the pitiful bellow of the trapped animal.

He guided his horse away from the slippery bank and stared at John who was covered to the waist with thick yellow mud. "Five of them stuck," he said in a despairing voice. "How will we ever get to California now?"

⤙ 2 ⤚

LATE IN the afternoon the sun's rays, slanting through thin clouds, hit Moses in the eyes as he looked across the river and saw that approximately a third of the wagons had reached the opposite shore. He realized it would soon be dark. He rubbed his face and slumped in the saddle, muddy, sweaty, and bone-tired.

"Come on, Moses! We need you down here."

He swung his mare around as he heard Dr. John calling, and walked her carefully down the soft bank.

"Watch this," Dr. John directed. "Captain Stephens has an idea. If it works, you can help us."

Captain Stephens and Caleb Greenwood climbed into a canoe. Dr. John handed the captain one end of a rope, tied the other end around the horns of their gentlest ox, and forced him into the water. While Mr. Greenwood paddled the canoe, Captain Stephens pulled the rope taut, guiding the ox. The frightened animal bawled as he stepped into deep water, then started to swim. Dr. John, Moses, and John Murphy drove more cattle into the water close behind him.

"It works! It works!" Moses yelled as they reached midstream, and the cattle kept going, swimming steadily as they slanted diagonally toward the opposite shore. Moses' and John's horses were swimming easily as they kept the cattle hurrying behind the lead ox. Moses' mare tired from the long swim, so he dismounted when they reached the shore and tied her to the nearest tree. He hurried back to help drive the cattle up the bank, and slipped in the mud, coating his pants to the knee.

Captain Stephens pushed back his broad-brimmed hat and stepped out of the canoe. He turned to Dr. John. "At least half the herd's across," he said wearily. "We'll make two camps. You are in charge here. I'll go back with the canoe."

Moses was stiff and cold. His arms ached from trying to pull out the mired oxen. He wanted to huddle close to the fire, but he knew the day's work was far from finished. He led his wet horse up to the wagon, rubbed her down, and tethered her where she could graze.

Elizabeth had a small fire blazing, and Moses walked toward it gratefully. This was only the beginning of the journey. If the other river crossings were as difficult, they would be lucky to reach Fort Hall by Christmas. He watched Dr. John coming toward him. His legs were caked with mud and he looked as tired as Moses felt.

"Help move the wagons into a circle, Moses," he said briskly. "Captain Stephens says the Otoes won't attack us, but they'll steal the cattle if we give them a chance. We can't afford to lose another ox—not after losing four already. We'll form a corral and keep the cattle inside tonight. We'll post guards, too. You and John Murphy can sleep first and take guard duty at midnight."

"You change those muddy clothes, right now, Dr. Townsend," Elizabeth ordered. "And you, too, Moses! You'll both have chills if you stand around here in the damp air in those wet boots and pants."

"Just a minute," Dr. John objected wearily. "Wait until we get the camp organized."

Moses and John Murphy helped move the wagons into the circle. When they finished, Moses sank down on a log across the camp from his wagon.

"I'm so tired I might have to crawl back," he complained. "What a day!" He broke off a small branch and scraped mud from the side of his boot.

John flopped down beside him with a long sigh. "If the rest of this trip is anything like this, we'll be gray-bearded old men before we reach California," he said impatiently. "I wish we'd get rolling."

"Me, too," Moses agreed as he rubbed his aching arms. "Say, John, are all of the people in your bunch of wagons related? I've never seen such a large family. I can't keep them straight."

John laughed. "Not all of them. Mrs. Miller is my sister. Martin junior and James Murphy are my brothers. They need wagons for their wives and children. Mr. Martin is James's wife's father, and Dennis Martin is her brother. Let's see. Counting our wagon, that's five."

Moses nodded, but still looked perplexed. "What about Ellen and Daniel?"

"My brother and sister," John explained. "Then there are Joseph Foster, John Sullivan, and his sister, Mary, who were neighbors of ours. That makes seven wagons."

Moses nodded again. "Mary is the girl with the copper-colored hair, isn't she?" He counted on his fingers. "Allen's wagon and ours makes nine. Captain Stephens' and Mr. Hitchcock's eleven. Mr. Greenwood's makes it twelve. A good, round number."

"You're right there. With that Mr. Calvin, Mr. Bray, and Mat Harbin on horseback and your hired man, we should be safe."

"You forgot John Flomboy and Ollivier Magnent. They've trapped and hunted, too," Moses said. "It'll be a hard trip for the women, anyway. I just hope it isn't too much for Elizabeth," he added, his voice betraying his affection and concern for his sister. "I wish some of the others would go with us like old Mr. Derby and his son, Perry, and Mr. Bean and Bill Higgins. Maybe they'll change their minds about Oregon."

He rubbed his arms again and looked curiously at John. "Why are you going to California, anyway?"

John leaned back against a tree trunk. "Well, my mother died of malaria right after we came to Missouri. So did three of my nieces. There wasn't even a priest to bury them. Dad grieved terribly." John stopped speaking and cleared his throat. "Then Father Hoecken came," he continued. "He told us about Spanish California where there are churches and schools. My father decided to leave Missouri then, and here we all are."

Moses had scraped the mud off one boot and started rubbing the other one across the grass.

"Say, John?"

"Yes."

"Do you know where California is—exactly?"

"Not exactly. Father Hoecken said it was west, but he didn't know how far. Do you know, Moses?"

"No." Moses stood up and stretched. "Not really. Dr. John says it's to the west, over the great mountains. Sometimes I wonder if California's really there."

"Father Hoecken said it was, and he'd know."

John climbed to his feet and they walked back to their wagons. The moment she saw him, Elizabeth ordered Moses to change his clothes, in a voice that indicated she would stand for no further delay.

Moses struggled slowly out of his wet boots and pants. He put on dry woolen stockings and dry pants, pulled on his spare pair of boots and jumped down from the wagon. He could smell meat and coffee, and he was suddenly so hungry that the aroma made his mouth water. He couldn't decide which was worse, his empty stomach or his aching muscles. Elizabeth held out a brimming plate of stew filled with chunks of meat, a thick piece of bread, and a cup of steaming coffee. Moses gulped down two helpings of stew and finished off the meal with a dish of stewed peaches. He went straight to his bed in the wagon, and was asleep almost before he pulled up the blankets.

It seemed only two minutes later when he felt someone shaking his shoulder. John Murphy was beside him, pulling at his arm.

"Midnight already?" Moses asked sleepily. He stretched, then winced from the twinges in his stiff muscles.

The two boys walked around the camp once and then sat by the low fire talking softly. "I'm sure there aren't any Indians within five hundred miles of us," Moses said. He could hardly keep his eyes open. His head drooped, then jerked as he fought to keep awake.

An hour later they made another round of the camp. The night was so dark the wagons were dim, ghostly shapes. The sky was covered with broken clouds.

Moses saw an occasional star, but the moon was hidden. The silence was broken only by an infrequent movement of the cattle, and the faint rustle of wind stirring the cottonwood trees.

"I never knew time to drag so," John complained. "No signs of Indians anywhere. This is silly. We could just as well be getting some sleep. Nothing is going to happen."

"Just sitting gets monotonous! I'm so sleepy I could sleep standing up. I sure wish we had something to do." Moses raised his rifle and drew a bead at the nearest tree.

John looked at Moses, yawned, and rubbed his red-rimmed eyes. "Now maybe, just maybe, we could do something. Moses, wouldn't it tear the place apart if the Indians did steal some cattle?"

"It certainly would liven things up, but there aren't any Indians around. We haven't seen or heard a sign of them."

"Captain Stephens said we wouldn't hear them if there were any, and if we can't hear them, no one else can, either. But we don't need Indians to steal cattle."

"You mean—"

John nodded and snickered.

"Whose cattle?"

"I don't know. What do you think?"

Moses hesitated. "Well, I wouldn't want to wake

Dr. John. He's up at night too much doctoring people. I don't think we should take your dad's cattle, either. How about John Sullivan's?"

"Good idea," John answered. "They're white. Easy to see."

They carefully tiptoed to the nearest wagon and lowered the tongue which rested on the wheel of the next wagon. A shrill squeak cut the silence. Moses held his breath, fearing the whole camp would be aroused, but no one stirred.

"They're sure to hear us," John whispered as they prodded the four white oxen through the opening.

"How far shall we take them?" Moses asked.

"Not too far. Just behind the closest trees. Remember, we'll have to find them again."

"That's not far enough," Moses said quickly. "Let's take them deeper into the woods."

They drove the cattle farther into the trees. Moses laughed. "This should be far enough," he said. "I'll go back and wake up Mr. Sullivan. You hide behind this log and scare him when he runs up."

"I can do better than that," John chuckled. "Just wait!"

Moses walked back to the camp quietly so that he wouldn't awaken anyone prematurely. He turned and looked for the cattle, but couldn't see them. He could barely hear the yoke ring clinking faintly in the still air.

He went into Mr. Sullivan's tent and shook his arm.

"Wake up," he whispered. "Your oxen are gone! We can't find them!"

John Sullivan scrambled out of his blankets and grabbed his pants. "Sound the alarm! Which way did they go?" he yelled, pulling on his boots. "I just knew those thieving Injuns would get the oxen!" He raced out of the tent and looked frantically to the left and then to the right. "Which way did they go?"

"I don't know," Moses answered, trying hard to keep a straight face. "I made rounds on the other side, and when I came back the wagon tongue was down and they were gone."

Mr. Sullivan put a hand up to his ear and leaned toward the trees. "Hear that? It's the yoke ring. Come on!" He ran toward the sound. Moses followed, staying well behind him.

As Mr. Sullivan reached the edge of the grove and climbed on a log to look for the cattle, John Murphy's gun sounded like thunder in his ears. Mr. Sullivan tumbled off the log and raced back to camp. "Injuns! Injuns!" he shouted. "Injun attack. They shot me."

The men poured out of the tents, guns in their hands. "What happened? Where are the Indians?" Dr. John shouted.

"I guess John Murphy scared them off," Moses answered in a solemn voice.

Mr. Sullivan hurried back toward the trees, followed by Moses who could barely keep from laughing. They heard the clinking yoke ring coming closer and met John Murphy driving the oxen back to camp.

The men decided to make certain that the wagon train was safe and scouted the small grove of trees for half an hour. The women clustered near the fire with blankets wrapped around them. They kept their sleepy children close beside them and hushed those who were crying.

"There's no sign of Indians," Dr. John told the women. "They must have been scared away. Go back to bed. There's nothing to worry about."

"Maybe you're not worried, but I sure am," John Sullivan declared. "I'm fastening the oxen to my wagon, and I'm sitting right here beside them the rest of the night. I'll keep my gun loaded and handy, too."

Moses and John grinned at one another as the sleepy travelers returned to their tents. Moses winked at John who smiled back as they sat down beside the fire. Neither one dared say a word.

There were still several long hours to go before morning. Moses found himself chuckling quietly as he circled the wagons. The sight of John Sullivan nodding over his rifle made him want to laugh aloud. Finally the camp began to stir as the sky paled. Moses yawned and walked eagerly to Elizabeth's fire as he smelled bacon and coffee.

As soon as Captain Stephens crossed the river with

the first wagon, Mr. Sullivan raced up to him and indignantly related his harrowing experience with the Indians.

Captain Stephens listened attentively and then turned and stared long and hard at Moses and John. He looks like one of those patriarchs from the Old Testament that the traveling preachers talk about, Moses thought. He felt a chill start at his neck and run down his back.

"First time I've heard of an Otoe attack in years," the captain said, his voice stern. "Can't understand it. But you're mighty brave and resourceful young men."

Moses didn't dare to look at John. He scuffed his boot in the dirt. "Well, Captain Stephens, we didn't do much," he said.

"No, sir," John joined in. "We didn't do much at all, and the excitement sort of made the night seem shorter."

"I'm sure of that!" Captain Stephens' voice was sharp. Then he paused and scratched his head. "Funny thing, though. Can't understand why the Injuns only picked on Sullivan's cattle and didn't take the rest. What's your answer to that, boys?"

"Well, sir," Moses paused between each word. "It was an awfully dark night."

"So it was. Go on!"

"Yes, sir. Well, it was awfully dark. Wasn't it, John?"

"It sure was," John agreed. "So dark that Moses and I could barely see one another's face."

"That's it," Moses said. "It was so dark the Indians couldn't see the brown cattle. Mr. Sullivan's cattle are the only white ones, and they were visible in the dark. That explains it, sir."

Captain Stephens' face was stiff. "Guess you two are not only good at finding oxen in the dark, but you're good at using your heads, too." He stared at them for another long moment. "Just make sure you don't use them to get into trouble."

John and Moses waited, not daring to say another word. The captain walked away. "Do you suppose we fooled him?" Moses asked uneasily.

"Not for a minute," John answered. "We're just lucky."

During the two days it took to get the rest of the company across the Missouri Moses and John herded cattle, raced their horses across the prairie in their free time, and avoided Captain Stephens. At last all the cattle, oxen, wagons, and people were on the opposite bank. On a cold, cloudy May morning the wagons rolled westward from the river, following faint tracks across the grass-covered prairie. Looking ahead Moses wondered how anyone could be certain of the route across the vast prairie stretching before them. He marveled as Mr. Greenwood moved forward without hesitation, ranging far in advance of the company, riding back to the lead wagon at intervals to give directions.

At noon the wagons stopped. The women served dinner while the men rested and the cattle grazed during the brief halt. Mr. Greenwood seemed to have no difficulty in finding desirable places for the noonings and for the night camps. There was always adequate water for the animals and good grass close to camp.

Moses found himself beside the guide one noon and decided to ask the questions that had been bothering him. "How do you know where to go?"

"It ain't hard. There's plenty of signs if you know what to look for," Mr. Greenwood answered. "Trappers and traders been over this trail for years. Plenty of wagons been this way, too."

"How many wagons have there been before us?"

"Don't rightly know. There's a train behind us now bound for Oregon. A big one. About a hundred wagons. We need to keep ahead of them or else our cattle will have mighty slim pickin's."

Several days later Moses and John had completed their share of cattle driving and were riding ahead of the train in the early afternoon with Mr. Greenwood and his sons, John and Brittain. They crested a slight hill and came to the banks of the Elkhorn River. Moses whistled when he saw the flooded river and turned anxiously to the grizzled guide. "How will we ever get across that torrent?" he asked.

Caleb Greenwood frowned and studied the swirling water. "It ain't going to be easy," he said. "That's the trouble with wagons. Men and horses, and even cattle can swim, but wagons can't. Have to get them over someway, though. Ride back, you two, and tell the captain we'll camp here tonight."

Moses and John turned their horses and hurried back to the company to deliver the message.

"What's the river like?" Captain Stephens asked, his long face looking more cadaverous than ever.

"It's almost out of its banks." Moses' voice shook with excitement and apprehension. "Mr. Greenwood said the cattle and horses could swim. The river's high and swift and awful muddy—just like the Missouri!"

Captain Stephens directed the wagon train to the campsite selected by Mr. Greenwood and then called the men together.

"We need a ferry," he said. "There's no boat out here. We'll have to make our own."

"Make one! How?" Moses burst out. He blushed and was annoyed with himself for interrupting when Captain Stephens swung around with an angry glare.

"We'll show you, boy. Right now you start unloading gear from your wagon."

Moses went to work as directed, piling boxes, tools, and the precious bolts of silk and satin, wrapped carefully in heavy brown paper, on the ground as Elizabeth and Dr. John handed them down to him. He glanced curiously at the captain's wagon. Mr. Greenwood and Captain Stephens had removed the wheels from the wagon and were stacking rawhides next to it.

"That's all," Dr. John said as he swung down from the wagon. He bent over the pile of supplies, hunting for tools.

The moment Dr. John turned his back, Moses slid around the corner of the wagon and started toward the captain. He had to know what was happening.

Captain Stephens and Mr. Greenwood stretched the rawhides around the wooden wagon box. They sewed and laced the hides together, overlapping the skins to make the box as watertight as possible.

As Moses edged closer, Captain Stephens looked up and saw him. "Don't be a slacker, boy!" he said harshly. "You scoot back and help."

Somewhat crestfallen, Moses hurried back to his wagon and helped Allen take off the wheels. "I just wish someone would tell me what's going on," he grumbled. "The captain called me a slacker. I was only trying to find out what they were doing."

"All the wagons have to come apart," Allen explained. "We must hurry so we don't lose too much time. Each day we lose now means a harder trip over the mountains. We don't want to get stuck in the snow."

"Couldn't we do it an easier way?" Moses asked. "We'll just have to put the wagons together again and reload them on the other side."

Allen shook his head. "The wagons will come apart fast, and the way Captain Stephens is organizing the crossing, we'll do all the ferrying and reloading tomorrow and be ready to roll again the following day. We'll be in Pawnee country then, Moses."

Tents were erected. The women cooked supper and extra food for the next day while the men and boys worked on the wagons. Even the small children were set to work, stacking the food supplies and blankets. Moses helped Elizabeth roll the clothes in blankets and piled up the supplies so they could be covered with the canvas wagon top.

"We can't afford to get anything wet, especially the food," she said, "and we had better hurry. It will soon be dark."

At sunup the first dismantled wagon and supplies were loaded into the makeshift boat, and Moses and Brittain Greenwood helped ferry it across the muddy river while the rest of the men drove the cattle into the water. They moved like a well-organized army with a task for everyone. The middle-sized girls watched the smallest children while the women helped the men load and unload. As soon as the pieces of the first wagon were unloaded, Moses and Allen Montgomery started putting them together. Despite all their care, some water had seeped through the rude boat, and the women spread blankets and clothing on the prairie grass to dry in the sun.

Moses realized it was a tremendous task and thought they would never be ready to go by the next day. At least the cattle would be well rested and fed. There was an ample supply of good grass and water. He walked along the riverbank, watching the makeshift ferry swinging in the current, wondering how soon they would reach buffalo country.

Dr. John called to him from the boat. "Moses? What makes you think you can loaf while the rest of us work like beavers? Get on your horse and ride out and watch those cattle. This side of the river is Pawnee territory. We can't afford to lose any cattle. Don't you ever think?"

Moses felt resentment flow over him as he rode with John Murphy to join Joseph Foster and Dennis Martin who were guarding the herd.

"Why us?" he grumbled to John. "I had planned to go hunting. I want to get the first buffalo, and we should be close to them. I can't wait to shoot one."

"Me, neither! Mr. Hitchcock says they're as big as elephants and shaggy and brown, and that the plains are covered with them as far as anyone can see. Between us, we should be able to supply ten meals for everyone in the company."

"Sure—if we ever get the chance, but all I've done

lately is guard cattle and put wagons together after taking them apart." Moses was still annoyed, thinking resentfully that Dr. John expected him to act like a man but treated him as if he were still a child.

The wagons rolled out on schedule the next morning, with Captain Stephens yelling harshly at the laggards to hurry.

"I hope we never have to take wagons apart again," Moses said to Allen as he mounted his horse.

"I don't believe we will," Allen said, going to the head of his teams. "Mr. Greenwood says the streams should be going down."

The company moved across the prairie, heading into Indian territory. Moses watched Mr. Greenwood and his sons canter off in advance of the train. He wished he could ride with them. He wanted to see Indians and buffalo. The snail-like pace of the oxen annoyed him. He snorted impatiently as Elizabeth exclaimed with delight and leaned from her saddle, trying to reach a cluster of wild rosebuds just beginning to show color.

Moses studied her slight, straight figure as she sat easily in the sidesaddle, riding her horse as if she were leading a parade. His anger and impatience faded, and he slid from his horse and cut the cluster of buds. He mounted again, rode up beside her, and held out the flowers. Elizabeth took them with a smile. He felt better as he turned his horse and rode out to drive the cattle.

About midmorning Moses saw John Greenwood gal-
loping toward the wagons, his hand held high.

"Hold up!" he shouted. "There's a Pawnee village
dead ahead!"

3

JOHN YELLED again, "Injuns! Dead ahead!"

The drivers brought the wagons to an abrupt halt. "Corral the wagons!" Captain Stephens shouted as he galloped toward John Greenwood. Moses started to follow and then turned and rode swiftly back to Elizabeth who was beside the wagon. He patted his guns—the shiny pistols Allen had made for him—as he swung down from his horse and raced to help Dr. John and Francis Deland unyoke the teams of oxen and drive them into the circle of wagons.

The corral was swiftly formed, with the tongue of each wagon resting on the rear wheel of the one in front. The precious oxen and horses were driven into the circle. Small children were placed behind trunks and boxes and ordered sternly to remain there. Men stood with their rifles raised, their wives beside them ready to reload or to shoot if necessary.

After a brief discussion with John Greenwood, Captain Stephens shouted to Moses, John Murphy, and

40

Allen Montgomery. "You three come with me. The rest of you men stay here. Keep alert and watch the cattle!"

Moses jumped on his mare's back, amazed and pleased that the captain had included him. They loped away from the corraled wagons, looking constantly from one side to the other, watching the horizon, peering suspiciously at the rolling prairie until they came to Caleb Greenwood who stood beside his horse at the bank of a small stream.

"The village is about two miles ahead," he said. "You can see it from the top of the next rise. It ain't right. Too quiet."

"A trap, maybe?" Captain Stephens asked calmly.

"Can't say," Greenwood replied, pulling at his beard. "We could circle around the village, but we'd go miles out of our way."

Captain Stephens considered the situation for a few moments. "I don't like the smell of things. If we detoured, we might run into an ambush. We'll take a look," he decided.

Greenwood nodded. He motioned for his sons to flank the riders and for Moses and John Murphy to bring up the rear. "You two ride like the wind for the company if we're attacked," he ordered. "Don't stop to help us. Give the warning!"

Moses watched Captain Stephens and Caleb Greenwood ride cautiously to the top of the rise. They looked ahead for several long moments, then waved Allen

Montgomery forward. John and Brittain Greenwood signaled from the flanks that all was clear. Moses took a deep breath, lifted his reins, and started up the hill, John Murphy beside him. They rode slowly, not daring to talk, watching Caleb Greenwood and his sons for any sign of alarm. The guide pulled his horse up when they were within a quarter mile of the village. He motioned for the flankers and Moses and John to join him.

"It sure ain't right," he said, studying the village.

"Why?" Moses asked. "Everything looks peaceful." He peered at the village drowsing in the sun. A circle of conical tepees, made of buffalo hides, stood close to the bank of a small creek. The village was as still as death. No children, no dogs, no horses. No sign of cooking fires. Not even a wisp of smoke.

"That's just the trouble," Mr. Greenwood answered. "No braves coming to meet us."

"Maybe they are lying in ambush," Moses suggested hesitantly. "Waiting to scalp us when we get closer."

"Nope." The guide was positive. "No Injun'd let us get this close if he was going to attack. He ain't about to allow us near his squaws and children. Come on. We'll ride in together."

The village remained quiet as they drew nearer. Moses rode alertly, his head swiveling from side to side, expecting a band of howling warriors to jump out at them any moment. His heart pounded, his mouth went dry as they trotted into the center of the village.

Small clouds of dust, kicked up by their horses' hoofs, floated in the air. Moses jumped as the wind rustled the shimmery leaves of nearby cottonwood trees. They reined in their horses and sat quietly in the saddles, peering at the tepees. Still all was quiet. No one came to meet them.

Caleb Greenwood swung down from his horse and strode into the largest tepee. He came out immediately, followed by an old Indian woman who blinked at the light as she haltingly replied to his questions.

"They are mourning their dead," Mr. Greenwood translated. "Sioux attack. Scalped most all their warriors. Ain't nobody left but women, children, and a couple of sick old men."

"Maybe Dr. John can help the sick ones," Moses suggested. "Shall I ride back after him?"

"We'll all go back and start the company moving," Captain Stephens decided. "There's nothing to fear from these Pawnees. If they allow Dr. Townsend to see the old men, maybe he can help them, but generally Injuns don't trust white men's medicine."

Moses galloped ahead, eager to reach Dr. John.

When Moses told him of the sick Indians, the doctor grabbed his black bag and started for the village, accompanied by Moses and Caleb Greenwood. "Does this mean the Pawnees won't be a danger to us?" Dr. John asked the guide.

"Yep, but we'd better watch out for the Sioux.

Wouldn't do to get caught between warring tribes. Them Sioux are the fiercest Injuns on the plains. They swoop down on their horses, and they wheel them horses like they was born riding bareback. They're a mean, treacherous bunch."

Moses followed Dr. John and Mr. Greenwood into the tepee and looked around eagerly while the doctor examined the two Indians.

An old man, so withered that he seemed nothing but a bundle of bones, his knees drawn up toward his chest, lay on a pile of buffalo robes. He turned his head away with a motion of anger and hauteur as Dr. John bent over him.

"There isn't much I can do for them," the doctor said to Mr. Greenwood. "I would expect this one to be screaming with pain. There's a growth in his stomach as big as a melon."

"Injuns ain't the screaming kind. They're proud people."

"Well, about the only thing I can do is leave some laudanum for him. It might help him to sleep a few nights, anyway."

He handed the drug to the old woman, told Mr. Greenwood to explain how to use it, and turned toward the entrance.

"Wait, Dr. John," Moses said hesitantly. "I don't see any food. They can't hunt, and they'll starve. Couldn't we share ours?"

"Perhaps we could spare a few—"

"Nope!" Greenwood interrupted decisively. "That ain't good sense. These Injuns will die anyway."

"We could try to help them," Moses muttered as he walked toward his horse.

"You're too impetuous, Moses," Dr. John said. "You have to consider this from the viewpoint of what is best for our own people. Greenwood's right. If we leave food here, some of us might die of starvation later."

Everything I say is wrong, Moses brooded, resentful again as they rode back to the wagon train. He was certain they could have spared a small amount of food, and he believed Elizabeth would agree with him, but he knew Dr. John would be annoyed if he brought the subject up again.

It was early afternoon by the time the wagon train had passed the village. The journey through the land of the Pawnees was easier than had been anticipated because Captain Stephens and Caleb Greenwood decided the cattle could be grazed more freely and allowed them to be taken farther from the wagons, but the men still had to stand the tiring night watches. Mr. Greenwood explained that, although this band of Pawnees had been decimated by the Sioux, there might still be Indians around to steal cattle if they were given the opportunity. Moses and John took their turn at the night watches and decided not to break the monotony of guard duty with jokes.

It was June now. The prairie was still green with spring grass and sprinkled with the bright blue of lupine. The cattle stayed fat, but with each successive day the sun's rays grew hotter and the trail became dustier.

Moses shot prairie chicken and antelope which made a welcome change from the bacon, pickled pork, and hard bread they ate, but he looked in vain for buffalo.

"I thought buffalo covered these plains," he said to John Murphy. "And I sure do want to shoot one. I'd even be satisfied to see one. I'm beginning to think they are mythical animals like the unicorns in one of Dr. John's books."

"Mr. Greenwood says we'll see them soon. I heard him telling my father that the buffalo flow across the prairie like a great tide, and that they trample everything in their path," John answered.

"They are supposed to be huge, shaggy beasts. I heard Mr. Hitchcock say that buffalo tongue is a fit treat for a mountain man. I hope we come across them soon. This is sure a tame trip. Sick Indians and no buffalo," Moses grumbled.

Three days later Moses was riding off from the side of the train to keep out of the dust. He heard a shout from Allen and looked to his right. Buffalo! Three of them! The huge animals with horns and strange humps moved ponderously across the prairie. Moses drew his rifle, kicked his horse in the flank, and rode straight for the nearest one.

His heart was thumping so hard from excitement that he could hardly hold his rifle steady. He gritted his teeth—bound and determined he was going to bring down the first buffalo.

The wagons halted, and the women screamed as the buffalo came steadily closer to them.

Moses took a deep breath, raised his rifle, and fired at a great shaggy bull. The buffalo tossed his head, snorted, and charged directly at the wagons. Moses fired again. Allen raised his rifle, aimed carefully, and pulled the trigger.

"He's hit!" Moses yelled, his voice shrill with excitement. The buffalo bellowed and snorted with pain, but he kept charging at the wagons.

Captain Stephens and Martin Murphy galloped down the line of wagons, shouting in an attempt to distract the wounded animal. The buffalo ran with his head lowered, straight at the Millers' wagon. Mrs. Miller shrieked and jumped from her seat.

Moses and Allen fired again and again. Moses was positive he had hit the buffalo at least four times. What did it take to kill a beast like this? There was time for only one more shot. Cold with fear, he aimed carefully. This one had to count! Suddenly the buffalo lumbered to a stop, slid to his knees, and fell to the ground with a heavy thud.

"He's not fifty feet from the wagons!" Allen shouted. "I thought he would never go down!"

Moses' hands were shaking on the reins as he forced his snorting, shying mare over to the carcass. Captain Stephens and the rest of the men came up to him.

"He's sure a big one. He looks like a mountain," Joseph Foster said admiringly.

"Yep," Mr. Greenwood agreed. "An old bull. He ain't no good. Too tough to eat."

"How many bullets did you use?" Captain Stephens asked.

"Why, I—I guess about ten, sir," Moses answered slowly.

"So did I," Allen said.

"Twenty bullets to kill one worthless bull! Don't you two realize we can't buy lead or powder out here on the plains? Next time make your bullets count." Captain Stephens glared angrily at Moses, swung his horse around, and shouted the order to start the wagons moving.

Moses couldn't believe that the buffalo wouldn't make a good supper. He and Allen decided not to butcher the animal, taking only the hump ribs and tongue to the Montgomery and Townsend wagons.

When they stopped for the night, Moses helped his sister and Francis build the fire and prepared to roast his meat. He tied it to the iron spit and watched carefully as the meat sizzled and turned a savory-looking brown. The aroma of broiling meat filled his nostrils and was wafted across the camp by the soft south wind.

"Mr. Greenwood doesn't know what he's talking about," Moses told Elizabeth. "Just smell that meat!"

"Just the same, I'll heat up these beans and side meat," Elizabeth answered. "Mr. Greenwood is a very wise man and is usually right. I've heard that he lived with the Indians for many years, so he should know when a buffalo is good to eat."

Moses speared off a hunk of meat, refusing the beans Elizabeth offered him. He sliced it with his knife, stuffed a chunk into his mouth, and started to chew.

"That does smell appetizing," Dr. John said. "Guess I'll try a piece."

Elizabeth watched Moses. "How is it?" she asked.

Moses nodded. He chewed and chewed, and then chewed some more. Finally he swallowed. "It's good. Wonderful flavor."

Elizabeth continued to watch with a smile as he started on the second bite. "Don't you want some beans before they are gone?"

Moses chewed vigorously and swallowed hard. He gulped as a big lump slid down his throat, and coughed until Dr. John hit him on the back. "Your beans are always good, Sis," he said when he could talk. "I wouldn't want to hurt your feelings by not eating any, but don't give me too large a helping."

"Well, I don't mind hurting your feelings by refusing a second helping of buffalo," Dr. John announced. "That meat is tougher than a worn-out mule. I would rather chew on my boots!"

Moses finished the beans and frowned sadly at the succulent-looking roast buffalo remaining on the spit. "It's not very tender," he said sheepishly, "but you must admit it has lots of flavor."

Early the next morning the train rolled on across the prairie. Moses never tired of watching the start. The camp bustled in the mornings, with the women cooking breakfast, and the men yoking the recalcitrant oxen and chaining them to the wagon tongues. Children were fed and dressed, horses were saddled, supplies were packed, fires stamped out as everyone hustled to be ready when Captain Stephens shouted the order to move. The sun grew hotter, and grass and fuel were becoming scarce, but Mr. Greenwood always managed to find a place with grass and good water to stop at noon. They rolled on, following the north bank of the Platte River day after day, fording small streams without difficulty. Elizabeth picked strawberries and wild peas to add variety to their diet and gathered an armful of wild roses and lupines. Dr. John laughed as she arranged them in a spare iron kettle and placed them on the tailgate of the wagon.

"You'll be getting out the damask napkins next," he teased.

Elizabeth flushed. "They made me think of home," she said.

Dr. John pulled her close. "You'll have a home again. The strawberries and peas are a good idea," he added seriously. "We need all the fresh food we can find. I don't want any of us to get scurvy."

Buffalo dotted the plains like raisins in a pudding. Many young calves and fat cows were shot, providing an ample supply of fresh meat for the entire company. Moses discovered another advantage of being in buffalo country when Mr. Greenwood selected a campsite for the night that had no trees nearby. Elizabeth wrinkled her nose in disgust when the old guide told the travelers to gather buffalo chips for their fires, but was forced to admit that the strange fuel burned steadily and made no difference in the cooking.

It wasn't until the middle of June that they sighted Fort Laramie. They had passed Court House and Chimney Rocks and wound around Scotts Bluffs, marveling at the rock formations, held spellbound by Caleb Greenwood's story of Hiram Scott who had been abandoned by the men assigned to stay with him and had died a lonely death at this place. When he noticed the distressed faces of the women, Mr. Greenwood hastened to add that the trapper had been buried by the great William Sublette who had found the skeleton the following year.

Elizabeth and Moses were riding just ahead of the

wagons when they first saw the fort. Moses leaned forward, straining his eyes to see it more clearly. Here they would rest, repair the wagons, and ask the traders if word had come back from California about the Chiles-Walker party. Moses glanced at Laramie Peak in the distance, then turned his attention back to the fort. As they drew nearer, he blinked hard and stared anxiously ahead. It seemed as if there were thousands of Indians crowding around the fort. He turned to Elizabeth. "Look at all those Indians!" he blurted. "Do you think the fort is being attacked?"

~⊀ 4 ⋊~

ELIZABETH stared apprehensively at the fort, her face pale. "Let's ride up and ask Captain Stephens and Mr. Greenwood," she said, doing her best to hold her voice steady.

Moses nodded, and Dr. John joined them as they rode forward to the head of the wagon train.

"There's sure a flock of Injuns. About as thick as crows in a corn field," Captain Stephens said. "I guess they're here to trade."

"Plenty of women and children with them," Mr. Greenwood added, matter-of-factly. "They ain't looking for trouble."

"We had better camp about half a mile away and set a strict guard around the herd, especially the horses," Dr. John suggested in a worried voice.

"Them Sioux got better horses than we got," Mr. Greenwood said. "Ain't no better horse soldiers than the Sioux. But we don't have to worry as long as we're here. We can start to worry when we leave. It might be a mite troublesome if we got caught by a band of warriors out hunting. They would scrunch us like we were lice."

Moses and Elizabeth looked at one another with troubled eyes as they turned back to the wagons. He patted her shoulder. "Don't worry," he said reassuringly. "We'll take care of you."

"Well, I'm not going to waste time worrying right now," Elizabeth answered in a brisk voice. "All I want is a bath and clean clothes and a chance to wash everything we own. Get the wagon as close to the river as you can, Moses."

"I suppose you're going to make me take a bath, too."

"You just know I am. Don't argue with me."

"I'll bet Mr. Greenwood doesn't take a bath."

"Probably not, although he could use one. But you can be sure you'll take one."

Moses knew Elizabeth would get her way, and he admitted to himself that the clean, clear water would feel good. He had some ideas that he wanted to talk over with Allen and Dr. John so he hoped that Elizabeth wouldn't assign him too many chores. For one thing, he wanted a chance to visit these Indians. The Sioux really had a reputation as fierce fighters. They were said to be able to charge with their horses just like a regular cavalry outfit. He wondered how they had learned such maneuvers, and he wanted to see some of the warriors. He also wanted to inspect the fort. Mr. Greenwood had told them it had been built by fur traders—by the great William Sublette.

But Moses was kept busy the rest of the day. Elizabeth directed him and Francis to bring up bucket after bucket of water so she could heat it and wash clothes and blankets. Looking at the wagon next to theirs, he saw that Allen's wife was scrubbing clothes, too. Women puzzled him. With a fort to explore and Indians to visit, they washed clothes and cleaned wagons.

He caught up with Allen on the way to the bank of the river. "Do you want to see the fort?" he asked.

"I sure do," Allen said. "Once I can get enough water to satisfy my wife, I'm on my way. I'm beginning to think that the river will run dry before these women are satisfied. My wife's planning to scrub out the wagon, too. Can't stop a woman from housecleaning. Not even when she's in a covered wagon out on the plains."

"Do you suppose these Indians do any trading?"

"I don't know." Allen shrugged. "Probably. Why else would they camp near a trading post?"

"I thought I would get some moccasins. I've almost worn out one pair of boots, and I noticed that the

Greenwoods all wear moccasins. They seem to hold up better than boots."

"The Greenwoods don't walk much, either. Still, moccasins are a good idea. I'll be barefoot before much longer." Allen glanced ruefully at his boots. The tops were cracked and the sole of the left one flopped with each step. "You know, Moses," he continued, "walking ten to fourteen miles a day is mighty rough on both boots and feet. I've tried tying the soles on with rawhide strips, but they wear through about the second mile. Right now I wish I knew something about cobbling."

The smells of supper were beginning to drift across the camp by the time Moses had carried up enough water to satisfy Elizabeth. She finished scrubbing the clothes and started to cook. "I'll do the other blankets first thing in the morning. Then everything will be clean," she said happily.

Dr. John sat down by the fire and balanced his plate on his knees. "There'll be a meeting right after supper," he announced. "Captain Stephens has a few things he wants to say. Then I think we'll have some music."

"And dancing, I suppose," Moses said in a resigned voice.

"That's an excellent idea. I know the women will enjoy it. An evening of relaxation will benefit everyone."

The hard work had sharpened Moses' appetite. He

started through his supper like a grasshopper in a rip-
ening field of grain. As he reached for a second piece of
corn bread, he glanced across the fire at Elizabeth. Her
face was flushed, and she pushed a stray curl back from
her forehead. She tapped a foot as if she could hardly
wait to start dancing.

"I suppose I'll have to dance with some of the girls."

"Moses Schallenberger! You act as if girls were
poison. It won't hurt you a bit to dance with them."

"Golly-whillikers, Sis! Girls are just a nuisance. Oh,
all right, if you say so."

Elizabeth hummed a tune as they walked over to
Captain Stephens' wagon where the rest of the company was gathering. Moses leaned against a wagon
wheel, staying at the edge of the group. Maybe he
could avoid the dancing if he kept out of his sister's
sight. As if she had read his mind, Elizabeth turned
back, pulled his arm through hers, and led him closer
to the fire.

The shadows lengthened over the wagon as the sun
set, and the fire threw flickering reflections against the
canvas tops. In the distance the hills turned a soft blue,
then slowly faded into gray. One star, then another,
twinkled as the sky darkened. Moses marveled at the
peace of the night, then his skin tightened as he heard
the bark of a coyote and the far-off howl of a wolf. The
prairie night appeared serene, but he knew that for the

unwary it could be as dangerous as a coiled rattle-snake.

Captain Stephens stood beside his wagon, arms akimbo, facing the emigrants. "We've come a far piece without trouble," he said sternly. "Don't want no trouble here, either, so listen to what I say about the fort and the Sioux. We'll camp here several days. It's a good place, and the cattle need to rest and graze. The women can cook up supplies, and I've noticed that they are already busy washing up everything in sight. Haven't seen such clean faces since we left Missouri." He paused while the men chuckled appreciatively. "It's a good chance to check over the wagons, too. I don't want anyone leaving here with as much as a loose bolt. Now about the Injuns. You can trade with them and visit their camp, but do it carefully and don't offend them. These Sioux are a proud, fierce people, and we don't want them angry at us. You can also buy supplies at the fort, but you'll find the prices high as mountains. Besides that, we shouldn't add weight to the wagons, so don't buy anything you don't absolutely need."

Captain Stephens looked slowly and sternly around the circle to make certain that everyone had understood him and then sat down in the shadow of his wagon.

"That's the most I've heard him say at one time since we started," Moses said to Allen Montgomery. "Talk about a man of few words. That's one who must be afraid it's going to cost him money whenever he opens his mouth."

"Yes, but he can sure snap out 'Do this' or 'Do that,' and mean it, too." Allen agreed.

Moses glanced longingly at the edge of the camp as a fiddler tuned up, and the first squares were formed for dancing. He started to drift toward the edge of the crowd, but Elizabeth gave him a sharp look. Might as well get it over with, he decided, and looked around for Mary Sullivan.

Mary smiled and nodded when he asked her to be his partner. They stumbled through the squares, with Moses wishing the caller wouldn't go quite so fast. He was always two steps behind everyone else. All this dancing every time there was a chance! Women seemed to think that this whole trip was a perpetual holiday with time for dancing every night. He would rather hunt buffalo or listen to the stories old Mr. Greenwood and Mr. Hitchcock told about the mountain men. The story Caleb Greenwood had related several nights ago about his Crow wife had really been a tale to hear. Batchicka—strange name for a woman, but when Mr. Greenwood said it with a voice so filled with pride that he almost choked, it seemed to mean something wonderful, like the still hush of the early morning just before the sun rose.

What a story it was! Greenwood had told them his eyes had failed. Batchicka loaded him and their five children into a canoe and started for Saint Louis where there were doctors who could fix his eyes. She took them past the Sioux warriors and pushed a Sioux brave into the water when he tried to steal their food. Even the treacherous Sioux admired such daring. They had laughed at the wet warrior and allowed the Greenwoods to continue. Batchicka and her family floated and paddled down the Yellowstone, down the mighty Missouri until, at last, they came to Saint Louis. There Batchicka—exhausted from the rigorous journey—died two months later. No wonder Mr. Greenwood's voice sounded clarion clear when he said "The Crow are the bravest of Injuns. My wife was a Crow."

Mary jerked his arm. "Stop woolgathering. You've swung me the wrong way the last two calls. What are you thinking about?"

Moses followed her over to the edge of the crowd. "I was thinking about the story Mr. Greenwood tells about his wife. Now there was a woman for you. Not like the ones around here who just think about fun and dances."

"What do you mean by that?" she snapped. "We do a lot of hard work, too, and don't have the fun of riding off hunting for buffalo all the time."

Moses looked down at Mary. She was rosy-cheeked,

her eyes bright. Her hair gleamed in the firelight. "I didn't mean to make you angry. I know the women work hard, but I was thinking about Mr. Greenwood's story and the dancing seemed foolish. Besides, I just don't like to dance."

Mary smiled. "Mr. Greenwood and his sons scare me. They look too much like Injuns, but I like to listen to Mr. Hitchcock. Do you think he really was in California seventeen years ago like he says? I thought only a couple of people had been to California."

"Maybe he was. I think sometimes the old mountain men start talking and just try to outdo each other. It's a wonder they don't claim to have been to Persia and the lands of Araby. But maybe he really was there. That man Walker, who started out with Joe Chiles and his wagons last year, was in California before. Mr. Hitchcock might have been with him."

"Did Mr. Walker and Mr. Chiles get the wagons through to California?"

"That's one of the things we should be able to find out at the fort. I'm surprised Captain Stephens and Mr. Greenwood didn't ask about it this afternoon, but I'm glad they didn't. Maybe I'll get a chance to go along with them."

Mary sighed and looked toward the west. "It seems like an awesome journey we're taking. They say the mountains touch the sky."

"Well, we'll soon know. The South Pass lies between here and Fort Hall, so we should learn what mountains are like soon. Right now I'm heading for bed. Tomorrow I'm planning to do some trading with the Indians."

"Would you do something for me, Moses?" Mary asked, her voice wistful.

"What?"

"I want some moccasins. My shoes aren't fit to wear. This afternoon several of the Injun women saw Sarah Mojave Greenwood and came over to talk with her. They gave her some of the prettiest moccasins I've ever seen."

"Do you have something to trade?"

"Nothing much. I have a hair ribbon I could spare and a string of beads. Walt Morton gave them to me before we left Missouri. Something to remember him by, he said. But I would rather have something comfortable on my feet to remember him by than the beads."

"I'll get them for you," he promised.

In the morning Moses accompanied Dr. John, Captain Stephens, and Martin Murphy when they headed for the Indian encampment. Moses looked at the clusters of tepees and moved just a step closer to Dr. John.

"These Indians are thick as mosquitoes after a flood," he said. "Will it be all right?"

"Of course," Dr. John answered impatiently. "They

came here to trade, and they'll be just as willing to trade with us as anyone else. I'm planning to get a couple of Indian ponies. I think they'll be hardier than ours, and they're certainly more accustomed to this kind of country. I don't want Elizabeth riding a horse that isn't surefooted through the mountains ahead of us, and I don't like the way her mare has been acting lately."

The circular Sioux encampment was almost as large as a city. They threaded their way through tepees covered with buffalo hides. Dogs ran back and forth, yapping and snarling, almost tripping them. Moses saw a squaw come out of a tepee, reach down for a fat puppy, and bash his head against a stone.

"Feast fit for a king tonight," Mr. Greenwood chuckled. "Some warrior will be well fed and happy."

Moses fought waves of nausea. "You mean they eat dogs?" he finally managed to ask.

"Ain't nothing better for a real feast," Mr. Greenwood answered.

Moses swallowed. "I could never eat a dog or anything like it."

"You'd be surprised at what you can eat iffen you ain't had any food for days. Anything that moves tastes good."

"Come on," Dr. John ordered impatiently. "We're here to trade."

The squaws gathered around the group as they walked into the center of the camp. They moved close to Moses, one pointing at his hair, another feeling the top of his arm. Moses pulled his arm away as the squaw laughed and jabbered at him.

"What's she doing? Measuring me or wondering if my hair would make a good scalp?"

"She's just saying you ain't finished growing yet. Says your muscles are mighty soft for so tall a boy," Caleb Greenwood translated.

"What's she mean—boy?" Moses swung around and glared indignantly at the old squaw who laughed again and then jabbered with the rest of the women.

"She says you've got pretty hair, though, and mighty nice eyes."

Moses wrinkled his nose in disgust. "I guess all women are alike. Can you barter a string of beads for a pair of moccasins, Mr. Greenwood?"

"That ain't hard. They like beads." He spoke to the Indians, using a combination of sign language and their own dialect. Moses tried to follow the gesturing and was wondering how anyone ever learned the motions and pronunciation when the old Indian woman laid down a couple of pairs of moccasins and started measuring them against his boots.

"Hey, what are you doing?" Moses jerked away and moved behind Mr. Greenwood. "They're not for me.

They're for Mary Sullivan. Tell her girls' moccasins. Just a little bit longer than my hand."

"Girls' moccasins, eh? Guess all girls ain't so bad. That Mary's got a right pert smile, ain't she?"

"Oh, I—I," Moses sputtered. "Her brother won't let her come near the Indians since that brave yelled at her yesterday. I guess he's afraid they want her red hair for a scalp."

Moses got the moccasins for Mary and then traded an extra knife for a pair for himself. He watched intently as Dr. John, aided by Caleb Greenwood, swapped three of their horses that were showing signs of wear for two Indian ponies. Dr. John managed to get the pinto he thought would make a good mount for Elizabeth, but it took much haggling and finally an extra horse. The Indian brave had put the horse through his paces, demonstrating his agility, and the pinto appeared to be mighty surefooted. The brave prized the horse highly, and it wasn't until Dr. John returned to the herd and came back with the third horse that the Indian agreed to the trade.

After leading the horses back to the herd, Moses and Dr. John turned toward the fort. "What are you planning to buy?" Moses asked.

"Probably nothing. Not at the prices these traders ask for their stuff. I want to inspect the place, and Captain Stephens and Martin Murphy think we might get some information about the wagon train that passed through here last year. If word has come back that Chiles and Joe Walker reached California with their wagons, we should be able to follow their trail with confidence."

Moses looked eagerly at the fort as they approached the gate in the wooden palisade surrounding the main buildings.

"I thought forts had soldiers. I don't see any here," he said in a disappointed voice.

"It's not that kind of fort," Dr. John explained. "It was built by Robert Campbell and William Sublette for the traders of their company, and for protection against the Indians. It was called Fort William at first."

With its square tower, and fifteen-foot-thick adobe walls, the fort looked impregnable to Moses. It had four two-story towers at the corners. As they went inside, he saw a big building with a wide porch. Caleb Greenwood led the party to the entrance.

They were greeted by a grizzled trader who lounged in a high-backed chair, his leg hooked over the arm. "So you finally got around to coming inside the fort. I suppose you people want to buy supplies."

"Nope," Mr. Greenwood said. "These people outfitted themselves pretty well before leaving Missouri. We just want to set and talk a mite and get some information."

"Well, information is free. What do you want to know?"

"What do you know about California? Any settlements there?" Dr. Townsend asked.

"There's a fort on the Sacramento River. Built by a Swiss named John Sutter who came through here a few years back. He calls it New Helvetia. We aren't so fancy. Just call it Sutter's Fort."

"Are there towns and schools?" Martin Murphy asked eagerly.

The trader shook his head and busied himself packing tobacco into a carved pipe. "I shouldn't think so," he answered finally. "It's a fort, a big one with a dozen guns that Sutter bought from the Russians mounted on the walls. I hear it's built of adobe brick and that Sutter has developed some farms nearby. He uses Injuns for workers."

"What have you heard about the wagons that started for California last year?" Martin Murphy asked. "Did they get through?"

"Why are you so curious about California?" The trader stared at them quizzically. "Aren't you people going to Oregon?"

"Nope." Caleb Greenwood lounged against the door and scratched at his greasy hair with black-rimmed fingernails. "Twelve wagons of us are heading for California."

"Twelve wagons! Across that desert and over those mountains? With women and children? You're foolish to consider such a journey. If you aren't scorched on the desert, you'll all freeze to death in the snow. There's no way to get wagons through to California."

✵ 5 ✵

Two DAYS later the train rolled away from Fort Laramie. The trader's statements about the impossibility of taking wagons across the mountains had been discussed interminably, with the emigrants chewing the alternatives over and over, like cows chewing their cuds. The owners of the twelve original California-bound wagons were still determined to attempt the difficult desert and mountain crossing. Some of the others who had almost decided to continue with the Stephens party were wavering, and the men talked about staying on the safe and known trail to the Oregon country.

Captain Stephens told the men to keep the wagons closer together so that they could quickly form a corral for protection in the event of an Indian attack. He ordered greater precautions, too, sending out several flankers and forbidding fires after sunset.

Mr. Greenwood and Mr. Hitchcock approved of the captain's defensive measures. "The Injuns probably know exactly where we are, and they won't attack at night anyway," Caleb Greenwood told the company. "Injuns ain't about to fight at night, but there ain't no use making it easy for them to sneak up on the camp and attack at dawn or steal horses."

Dr. John nodded. Elizabeth, who had been somewhat apprehensive about the Indians after seeing the large band at Fort Laramie, looked relieved. "We're fortunate to have a man as capable as Captain Stephens in charge," she told Moses. "Everyone in this company gets along well and takes orders. It seems to me that's important because we must be able to depend on one another if we are to get through safely."

Paul Derby objected. "I don't agree! Stephens is just an old granny who likes nothing better than to give orders and make people miserable. The nights are icy cold. I'm not going to freeze just because he's afraid of his shadow."

Moses didn't say a word. He knew Mr. Derby was still determined to leave the company at Fort Hall and go to Oregon as he had planned from the beginning. Mr. Derby was a cantankerous old man who had argued with Captain Stephens about the rules ever since they had left Council Bluffs. He complained about the heat, the dust, the flies, the water, the campsites, and the cold. No one would miss him, Moses decided, but they would miss his son, Perry, an amiable, cheerful young man who did more than his share of work.

About midmorning Moses decided he had better walk part of the day so his horse wouldn't become footsore. They were in rough, dusty country and the trail, still following the Platte, was rocky. When he heard the order to stop for the night, he helped Elizabeth gather buffalo chips and sage so that she could cook supper before it was time to put out the fire.

When supper was ready he stretched his legs in front of the fire, balancing his plate on a rock. "You're on watch tonight, aren't you, Dr. John?" he asked his tired, dust-covered brother-in-law. "Do you want me to take your turn? You've been up a lot lately taking care of sick people."

"No, thanks," Dr. John said. "I'll do my share. You're skinny enough, and you need your sleep. I do wish you would get some meat on your bones."

Moses laughed. "You can't say I don't eat enough." He held out his plate for a second helping.

The sun sank slowly behind the mountains and the shadows lengthened around the wagons. The fires were put out and the twilight deepened into darkness. Moses listened as the howl of a far-off coyote drifted through the air.

"Time to make a check of the camp," Dr. John said, with a sigh as he reached for his rifle.

"I'll walk around with you, if you don't mind," Moses said. "I'm not sleepy yet."

Dr. John smiled. "I would appreciate your company."

Moses glanced at him a couple of times as they circled the wagons, looking to see if the herd guards were alert.

"Is something bothering you, Moses?" Dr. John asked.

"Sort of."

"If it will help to discuss it with me, I'm ready to listen."

"I keep thinking about that trader's words. That we'll all die in the snow. That no one knows what happened to Chiles or Walker."

"I, for one, have no intention of dying in the snow or on the desert. I'm positive we'll get through safely," Dr. John stopped talking suddenly, staring at a small campfire beside Mr. Derby's wagon.

"Derby, didn't you hear the captain's orders?" he asked angrily as he grabbed a stick and scattered the fire.

"Leave my fire alone! Stephens is an old granny with milk for blood."

Moses watched while Dr. John stamped on the remains of the fire. "Don't do that again, Derby," he ordered sharply and started off to check the remainder of the camp. Moses waved his hand and turned back toward their own wagon. He could hear Mr. Derby muttering to himself as he walked away, then he saw the reflection of the fire flickering again on the side of the wagon in front of him. Moses turned. Dr. John was running toward Mr. Derby.

"Do you want to get us all killed?" he yelled. "Put that fire out right now!"

"No!" Mr. Derby snapped. "I won't and it won't be healthy for you to do it, either."

Dr. John didn't say another word. He grabbed Derby's water bucket and emptied it over the fire. After scattering the coals, he turned to the obstinate man. "You light that fire again tonight, and I'll put it out by rolling you in it!"

That settles it, Moses decided. He walked back to the wagon and crawled into his blankets. Relieved of his worries by Dr. John's optimism, he went to sleep without difficulty.

The next morning Moses helped Francis yoke their oxen so that Dr. John could sleep as late as possible. As they finished breakfast, he saw Mr. Derby and Captain Stephens coming toward their wagon. Derby was nothing but a troublemaker, he thought, turning reluctantly to awaken Dr. John.

"There he is!" Mr. Derby shouted as Dr. John came out of the tent. "Now you tell the captain precisely what you did with my fire last night."

Dr. John stared contemptuously at Mr. Derby. "I put it out—twice," he said quietly. "Then I told you if I had to put it out again, I'd do it by rolling you in it."

"Suffering catfish!" Captain Stephens roared. "Is that why you dragged me all the way over here? Well, if you light another fire after dark, Derby, I'll personally help Dr. Townsend roll you in it."

"You're nothing but a bunch of scared grannies! I won't lower myself by traveling with a crowd like this." Mr. Derby turned, stamped over to his wagon, and drove it out of line.

"Move out!" Captain Stephens shouted, and the caravan started, with Mr. Derby staying about half a mile behind the other wagons. He's an old mule, Moses thought, as Derby continued to stay behind the company for a week, camping about the same distance away that he traveled, but he was wise enough to put out his fire at sunset.

It was almost July. The trail was hot, dusty, and rougher each day. Their pace slowed imperceptibly although Captain Stephens constantly reminded the travelers of winter's approach and urged them to more speed.

One noon Moses noticed that John Greenwood wasn't riding ahead with his father, but remained close to the wagon. Moses hadn't seen John's young wife for several days. He was suddenly curious and walked over to Mary Sullivan who sat beside her wagon fanning her flushed face with her sunbonnet.

"What's the matter with the Greenwoods?" he asked. "It's queer to see John staying behind with the wagons."

"His wife's sick," Mary explained. "John Murphy hasn't been feeling well, either. He's riding inside the wagon today, too."

"What's the matter?"

"It appears to be the ague. Anyway, it's some kind of chills and fever."

"I thought we had left that behind in Missouri," Moses said. A frown creased his forehead. "I sure do hope Elizabeth doesn't come down with it."

"You're so busy looking for buffalo that you wouldn't notice a thing if half the people around turned green," Mary answered. "Dr. John's been making Elizabeth rest a lot and he's been taking care of Mrs. Greenwood and John Murphy, too. If you want to know about the sick people in the company, why don't you ask your brother-in-law? After all, he's the doctor."

Moses flushed. "Well, we need fresh meat, and someone has to do the hunting. I bet I kill my share of buffalo before we leave the plains." He turned and walked away from Mary. Girls! Always criticizing. A fellow could never do anything right as far as girls were concerned. That Mary Sullivan. Her red hair, gleaming brightly in the sun, didn't begin to compensate for that nasty temper.

Moses' back was poker-straight as he hurried to his own wagon where Elizabeth rested in the shade.

"Where is Dr. John?" he asked. Elizabeth was surely all right, he decided. She was thinner, but her smile was as bright as ever as she motioned him down beside her.

"In the Greenwoods' wagon," she said.

Moses sat next to Elizabeth for a moment. Mary Sullivan's words still rankled and he decided to go over to the Greenwoods' wagon. Maybe he could carry water for them.

Dr. John swung down from the tailgate as Moses approached. He turned and lifted down Sarah Mojave who sobbed and squirmed, fighting to get back inside the wagon.

"Here, Moses," Dr. John called. "Take this youngster back to our wagon. Tell Elizabeth to keep her there."

"What about the other girl?"

"She's with Mary Sullivan."

Dr. John's face was grave. He sighed and straightened his shoulders as he picked up his bag. "I'm going to take a look at John Murphy before we start."

"Are they awfully sick?"

"John's getting better. I don't know how—" He broke off, glancing at Sarah Mojave. "Get her over to Elizabeth," he ordered. "I'll talk to you later."

Sarah's sobs ceased. She twisted and darted away from Moses. He leaped after her, grabbing her just before she scrambled back into the wagon.

Holding her firmly by the arm, he turned and hurried to Elizabeth. "I know how you feel," he said gruffly to the child, "but you must do as Dr. John says. Now stay here and don't give Elizabeth any trouble."

Elizabeth scooped Sarah into her lap and brushed a tangle of hair back from the child's face. "She'll behave, Moses. Don't be so rough with her."

Moses started to protest, then turned to the teams as he heard the signal to start. Francis was herding cattle and with Dr. John busy with sick people, he would have to drive the oxen.

As he trudged beside the team, he glanced back at Elizabeth who held Sarah's hand as she walked close to the wagon, trying to stay in the shade. It was hot! So hot that Moses felt as if he were an egg frying in a pan. As he wiped sweat away from his eyes, he wondered if people's brains could boil. Then he felt ashamed. Here he was being sorry for himself because he was walking and the sun was hot, when John Murphy was sick and, as far as he could tell from Dr. John's troubled face, Mrs. Greenwood might be dying.

Sarah Mojave. It was an odd name, he thought. The Greenwoods were an odd bunch. Mr. Greenwood seemed much too old to be the father of such young children. He wondered what would happen to Sarah if young Mrs. Greenwood died.

He plodded ahead, shading his eyes from the sun, watching Elizabeth anxiously throughout the long afternoon. When the signal finally came to stop for the night, he helped unyoke the oxen as Elizabeth put Sarah to work assisting her with supper.

Watching her solemn face as she pushed her food around the plate while they ate supper, Moses wondered if the little girl ever smiled.

"She'll sleep with us tonight," Elizabeth announced. "I'll make a bed for her next to mine."

Dr. John nodded as he hurried with his supper. He straightened wearily as he turned to go back to the Greenwoods' wagons. "I'll be with Mrs. Greenwood if anyone else needs me," he said.

Moses walked a few steps with him. "How is she?" he asked quietly.

Dr. John shook his head. "I really don't know, Moses. There's not much to be done for ague except wait and hope the fever will break."

As he turned toward the wagon, Moses hoped that the next day would be cooler. He was so tired that he twisted and turned, pulling his blankets into a tangle before he finally fell asleep.

Peering out of the wagon at daybreak, he saw Dr. John sitting before a small fire, his head bowed. Moses pulled on his pants and boots and hurried out to him.

"Are you awfully tired?" Moses asked falteringly, wondering about Mrs. Greenwood. "Were you up all night?"

Dr. John nodded.

Moses reached for the coffeepot, filled it, and set it on the fire. He stared at his brother-in-law for a long moment, then blurted out the question. "How's Mrs. Greenwood?"

"She died," Dr. John answered, pounding his knee with his fist. "I did my best, but—"

Elizabeth spoke from behind them. "Don't do that, John." She bent and held his hands tightly in hers. "You always tear yourself to pieces when you lose a patient, and you know you've done everything that could be done. Now come with me. You need to rest." She urged him to his feet and led him to the tent.

"How's John Murphy? You didn't say," Moses asked anxiously, following them.

"He's as good as new."

Moses smiled for the first time that morning, then

immediately sobered as he saw Sarah Mojave's forlorn face. She came out of the tent and crept over to the fire. Moses pulled her close to him. "We'll have flapjacks in a few minutes," he said. "Are you hungry?"

✎ 6 ✐

LATER that morning Moses watched as the men dug a grave and buried John Greenwood's young wife. He wondered if there would be other graves before they reached California. Graves with only a few hurried words said over them, with not even a rude cross or stone for a marker.

Elizabeth stood beside him, wiping a tear from her cheek. She clutched his arm as the dirt was shoveled back and shuddered when Captain Stephens and Mr. Hitchcock drove their wagons back and forth over the small mound.

"No!" she said in a choking voice. "We should put up a marker with her name on it."

Dr. John shook his head. "Captain Stephens says the Indians would find the grave if we marked it," he explained gently.

Sarah Mojave was beside herself with grief. Elizabeth did her best to console the child, but Sarah pushed her away with stiff, jerky motions. Moses knew just how she felt. He remembered feeling the same way when his own parents had died—lost, deserted, angry at a world that would hurt him this way. He had been just about the same age, too. He realized that John Greenwood's wife had been a mother to Sarah. She had taken care of the girl the way Elizabeth had taken care of him. Whatever would he have done without Elizabeth and Dr. John? He always felt sorry when Dr. John lost a patient. It seemed as if he lost something of himself, and it took days for him to regain his usual jovial spirits. Dr. John was the smartest, most genial man in the company, Moses thought proudly, even though he did have a tendency to lecture whenever he had an opportunity.

Moses heard Captain Stephens give the order that started the wagons, and he mounted his horse gladly, anxious to get away from the grave, hoping with all his heart that they wouldn't have to bury anyone else.

It was his turn to drive the herd. It was hot, dusty, tedious work, and they moved only a few miles before noon. Moses stretched out under the wagon, hunting for a patch of shade as soon as he finished eating.

"Hey, the camp!"

Moses scrambled out, almost tearing his pants on the wheel, alarmed at the shouting. Allen Montgomery and

Martin Murphy, who had been out hunting, galloped toward the camp.

"Big band of Sioux!" Allen shouted. "About five miles off."

"Any women with them?" Captain Stephens asked calmly.

"We didn't see any, but we didn't stop long to look, either."

"Allen, ride back and tell that idiot Derby he had better close up unless he wants to be a lone scalp," Captain Stephens ordered. "Maybe he'll learn now," he added with a chuckle.

"Aren't you worried? Won't they attack us?" Moses asked, amazed that the captain could laugh when they were in danger.

Captain Stephens shook his head. "No. They must know we're here. I figure they won't bother the company, but they might be attracted by the easy picking Derby would make."

John Murphy walked up to the group. "Get any buffalo, Allen?"

"No. We didn't see any. Just lots of Indians."

"Too bad. We need meat," Captain Stephens said.

"I bet Moses and I could get plenty of meat," John announced. "I was cheated out of the hunts when I was sick. I bet the two of us can bring back all the buffalo we need."

"We sure do need fresh meat, but what makes you boys think you're so good?" Captain Stephens asked sternly.

Moses drew himself up straight, annoyed at being called a boy. "We're good hunters and good shots. I bet we can bring back enough buffalo to supply the whole company."

"And plenty to spare, too," John Murphy added.

"Go ahead, but keep away from the Injuns. Just remember that when you boast about your hunting and are willing to bet on the results, you had better make good." Captain Stephens gave permission with a forbidding stare and a twinkle in his eye.

Moses and John started off early the next morning. Moses wore his prized gun belt buckled around his waist. He patted the pistols proudly. No one had better guns, he thought with satisfaction. They headed left, and after riding for an hour, spotted a herd of buffalo close to the river.

"Look at the size of that herd!" John said. "There's meat enough on the hoof for a dozen companies."

"They're starting away." Moses pointed to an old bull on a nearby hill. "He gave the alarm. They're smart beasts. They put out guards."

"Come on! We'll follow them."

Moses and John trailed the herd for more than an hour, but couldn't manage to get close enough to shoot at a fat cow. They turned away from the river and found another herd, but still couldn't get near enough to shoot.

At midafternoon they crested a gentle rise and saw a third herd grazing about a mile away. They rode toward it cautiously, making a half circle so that they could approach the animals from upwind.

Moses grinned as they rode nearer the herd. This time they would make it! Just a few more yards and he could be certain of bringing down a fat cow.

A shaggy bull, grazing about two hundred yards in advance of the herd, suddenly bellowed the alarm. Again the herd moved away from them.

"I don't see how anyone ever manages to kill a buffalo," Moses said angrily. "I'm tired and I'm plenty disgusted, and it's almost sunset."

"We haven't even been close enough to shoot once," John complained.

"Don't you think I know that?" Moses answered impatiently. "We'd better start back before it's dark."

"Yes, but— Oh, golly!" John checked his horse and looked at Moses. "It's going to be hard to explain that the buffalo had guards out, and we didn't get a single shot."

"It's going to be harder yet when they ask where all the meat is. I can hear them talking now about the mighty hunters who bet they could kill enough meat for everyone and came back empty-handed. You know, John," Moses continued in a low, serious voice, "we should have kept our mouths shut until we had shot the buffalo."

"I guess you're right. If we hadn't talked about buffalo, we could have shot antelope. I've never seen so many of them in one day."

"Me neither. But we said buffalo, and if we bring back antelope, we'll hear remarks about the funny-looking buffalo without humps."

"But maybe they won't laugh quite so hard." John patted his horse on the neck, and they turned reluctantly toward the camp.

Antelope grazed peacefully in every direction. The graceful animals didn't seem to be the least afraid. "It's as if they knew we weren't hunting them," Moses said, exasperated.

"They are so close, I'm afraid they'll bite." John cowered in mock terror as the nearest antelope calmly watched them. He lifted his rifle, aimed, and fired.

The animal fell in its tracks and the rest of the herd scattered. "Good shot," Moses said. "There's no point in leaving the meat for the wolves."

They dismounted and began butchering the antelope. "At least we'll go back with something, and this meat looks fat and tender," John said bending over the carcass. He straightened up for a moment as he swiped at a mosquito on his forehead. "Hey, Moses!" he shouted. "Watch the horses! They're straying."

"I'll get them," Moses volunteered. "You finish up here."

Moses laid his gun belt, pistols, shot pouch, and powder horn on the grass beside his rifle. Then he ran across the prairie after the horses. He fought his way through the waist-high grass and grabbed the reins.

"You idiot," he said, rubbing the nose of his brown mare. "I didn't think you would leave me out here." As he turned back, he noticed that the blanket had slipped off John's horse. He walked back slowly, searching for the blanket. Golly-whillikers, where could it be, he wondered, as he looked through the long grass.

"Hey, John!" he yelled. "Your blanket's gone. Better come and help me look for it."

Moses continued to hunt for the missing blanket, trying to retrace the horses' steps through the long grass. John raced up to help with the search.

"This grass is too long," he complained. "The blanket would be easier to see if the grass was short and clumpy like the grass we were in a couple of days ago."

"But then we wouldn't have seen the buffalo and antelope herds. They're here because the grass is so good." Moses followed the tracks that the horses had made and finally found the blanket. He handed it to

John. "Better fasten it tighter," he advised. "Let's load the meat and get back to camp before it's so dark we lose our way."

They turned around and started back to pick up the meat.

"It was over there." John pointed to the left.

"No. We were closer to the river," Moses said and turned to the right. They rode about a quarter of a mile and then worked their way back to one another.

"We must be right by it," Moses said, puzzled.

"Let's go this way," John answered and turned again to the left.

"We have to find the place. My pistols and gun belt are there."

"Yes, and both rifles, too."

They made another wide sweep across the prairie without finding the body of the antelope. Moses' heart thumped as the first stars twinkled in the darkening sky. He just couldn't lose his rifle and the pistols. What would Dr. John say? What would Allen say? He looked at John in dismay. "It's too dark to search any longer tonight. We had better get back to the camp," he said. His voice quavered, and he swallowed hard, hoping John wouldn't notice.

"You're right. We would have to fall over the carcass to find it now. But what are we going to say?"

Moses slumped in the saddle, thinking of the guns.

Why had he taken them off, and how was he going to face Allen? What could he say?

"Well, suggest something!" John said. "We can't ride back without our guns and powder, and without buffalo and not even any antelope, and not say a word. They'll laugh at us from now until we reach California."

Moses slowed his horse to a walk. He wasn't in any hurry to get back to the camp. "I'm trying to think of something. How about telling them we were attacked by Indians?"

"That's a great idea!" John answered. "We can say we lost our guns in the fight and we killed four of the Indians, and we were lucky to get away alive."

"Maybe we could say we killed six Indians." Moses' face brightened for a moment. Then he slumped in the saddle. "You know that won't work. They'll never believe we killed even one Indian and got away."

"I guess not. We'd better think of something else," John answered. "Couldn't we say that the Indians ambushed us and robbed us of our guns and powder? We could say that we escaped by sneaking to our horses, and we rode furiously all day and then hid by the river until dark, and that we are lucky to be alive."

"Or maybe we could say that the Indians let us go after taking the guns and the belt and powder," Moses suggested. "Come on. Let's find the camp."

He touched his horse with his heel, and they increased their pace. "There's the camp now," Moses announced, after half an hour of riding. He pointed at the shadowy circle of wagons, looked at John, and pulled on his reins, forcing his horse to stop.

"We'll never get away with it, John."

"Why not?"

Moses turned in his saddle and smiled wryly. "Look at us. No signs we've been in a fight at all. Besides that, who will believe that the Indians let us keep our horses?"

"We could get down and rough each other up," John suggested. "Then it would look more real."

"It might look more real, but it just wouldn't go over. You know it wouldn't. Indians would never rob us and let us go. Besides that, I've never been able to look Dr. John in the face and get away with a lie."

"And besides that," John answered dismally, "there's Mr. Greenwood and Captain Stephens. The captain would know just by looking at us. He knew all about that trick we played on John Sullivan. We were lucky to get away with it, but I don't think we could get away with this story."

Moses was silent for a moment. His face burned at the memory of the foolish joke they had played. It had seemed like a great stunt at the time, but now, out on this lonely prairie, it seemed stupid—a childish trick.

"I know very well we wouldn't. There's nothing to do but face the music." Moses straightened his shoulders. "Golly-whillikers, I'm hungry. Let's hurry and get it over with. But I sure do wish I hadn't taken off those pistols."

∽✦ 7 ✦∼

HE HAD better hold his chin high and keep his mouth shut tight, Moses told himself as he rolled up his blankets the next morning. Dr. John, his face as dark as a thunderhead, had lectured him for ten minutes about carelessness. Elizabeth had shaken her head sadly, and Allen had given him a wry smile and a clap on the shoulder when he had explained how sorry he was about losing the guns.

He hadn't escaped the jeering remarks, either, about the mighty hunter who had come back without game and without guns. Moses had kept quiet, almost biting his tongue a couple of times, knowing that excuses would only make matters worse.

His brother-in-law was standing beside the fire when Moses came reluctantly out of the tent. Dr. John handed him a rifle.

Moses took the gun with a look of gratitude. "Thanks

very much," he said in a low voice. "You know I do feel just awful about losing my guns."

Dr. John was curt. "That won't help. Hurry and eat. Then some of us will go back with you. Maybe we can find the guns."

Moses and John Murphy led the men back toward the spot where they had shot the antelope. They spread out and hunted for several hours through the tall grass that rippled under a slight breeze from the south. Finally, as the sun grew higher and hotter, Dr. John straightened up and called in the search party.

"There's no use," he said. "We could look for weeks without finding the guns. We could be within two feet of them and not see them."

They gave up the search and rejoined the wagons. Moses looked back with regret at the green prairie where his pistols were hidden. If only he hadn't taken them off!

For the next two days the company moved slowly along the banks of the Platte River and then followed the Sweetwater, climbing so gradually that it didn't seem like a climb at all. They ate almost nothing but fresh meat, trying to save their supplies of flour. Three or five men, detailed as hunters each day, kept the entire company supplied with game.

Mr. Greenwood announced during one nooning that he thought they should camp on the Sweetwater for several days and lay in enough meat to last until they reached California, because buffalo would soon be scarce. Since they had stopped at a suitable place, Captain Stephens decided they might as well remain there. Grass and water were plentiful, and the hunters could start out early with rested horses.

Moses was awake before daybreak. With John Murphy, Allen Montgomery, and Joseph Foster, he swung up on his horse at the first sign of daylight and started out after buffalo, grimly determined that this time he was going to kill more than his share. After riding for several miles, the group of men spotted two herds.

"Which one do you think we should go after?" Moses asked Allen.

"That's hard to say." Allen hesitated, studying the buffalo dotting the plains. "Maybe we had better split up. That will give us a double chance."

Moses and Allen decided to follow the herd on the left. John and Joseph rode off to the right.

"I bet we come back with more meat than you do," Joseph shouted with a laugh.

"You don't catch me making bets about what I'm going to do before I do it," Moses answered ruefully, his face red. "Not after the last hunt I went on."

Moses and Allen trailed the herd for hours. It seemed to Moses that the buffalo drifted ahead of them like ghosts. Just when he thought they had a chance to get close enough to shoot, the big beasts would move and, for all their huge size, they moved just fast enough to stay out of rifle range. Late in the afternoon the herd headed into country that was mounded and rocky.

"We'll get them now. We can crawl up behind the rocks, and if we stay upwind, they won't spot us," Allen said hopefully.

Moses nodded. He was tired, but determined that this time he would prove himself to be a good hunter. They crawled slowly and carefully to the top of a mound, watching their rifles so the barrels wouldn't get dirty. They crept around the side of a big rock and, scarcely breathing, studied the herd grazing peacefully just below them. They started to crawl forward then discovered, directly in front of them, a hulking bull lying next to the rock.

Allen jerked Moses back and leaned close to his ear. "He's asleep," he whispered. "Do you think we can get past without waking him?"

"We must." Moses' legs trembled as he looked at the bull. He took a deep breath to steady himself and moved away from the rock. He crept carefully around the bull, worried that the animal might scent him. He would have to pass within a few feet of the bull's head. He crawled on his elbows, pulling his rifle down carefully each time he moved. The bull snorted as he came closer. Moses froze, his forehead wet with sweat, wondering if the buffalo would trample or gore him if awakened suddenly. He hoped buffalo didn't roll over when they were sleeping. If this one did, he would be crushed as flat as a flapjack.

After a few moments, Moses moved again, snaking past the bull. He went on for a few more yards until he judged that the animal could no longer get his scent, and stayed quietly on the ground, waiting for Allen to join him.

As Allen crept cautiously past him, the bull jerked, snorted, then suddenly leaped to his feet and dashed in the direction of the herd.

Allen jumped up and fired, missing the animal. "Why didn't the old beast sleep?" he yelled in disgust. The herd milled aimlessly, apparently not frightened by the shot, and then moved away again. Allen and Moses went back for their horses, mounted, and followed the buffalo, grimly determined that this hunt wouldn't be a failure.

"It'll be dark soon," Moses said. He was tired and disgusted. "Do you think we'll ever get close enough to shoot at one?"

"I'm just mad enough to chase them from here to California and back," Allen answered. "And I'll never believe anyone who calls animals dumb. These are mighty smart beasts. No wonder you and John Murphy couldn't get a shot at them."

"Look!" Moses pointed at the herd. "They're stopping. They must have found water."

"Let's try something different. We can leave the
horses here and crawl up through that depression."
Allen pointed to a shallow ravine lined with grease-
wood. "We'll stay low."

They crawled forward on their bellies, trying not to
make a sound, to within two hundred yards of the herd.

"We should be closer, but we had better chance it,"
Allen whispered. "It's almost dark. If we wait any
longer, we won't be able to see to shoot."

Moses nodded. They stood up and aimed at the nearest cow. Both of them fired at the same time. The cow
fell without taking a step.

"That's queer. They didn't run." Moses watched the
animals, puzzled by their reaction. The herd gathered
around the fallen cow. Moses and Allen sank down behind a bush and reloaded their rifles. They walked
slowly toward the herd, shooting as fast as they could
fire and reload. Seven buffalo tumbled to the ground.

"I guess that's all," Allen said matter-of-factly as the
frightened herd scattered. "We hit some good ones,
anyway. Let's get up there."

Moses could barely restrain himself. He wanted to
shout. He could hardly keep from capering across the
prairie. He skipped for a couple of steps as he followed
Allen toward the fallen cows. Allen stopped so sud-

denly that Moses almost ran into him. An old bull remained near the dead cows, bellowing and pawing at the ground.

"What's he doing?" Moses shouted.

Allen stared, puzzled. "Never saw a bull do that before," he said. He raised his rifle and fired. The animal bellowed with pain and then dropped beside the dead cows.

When they reached the first cow they had shot, they stopped to inspect the carcass. The bullet holes were only two inches apart.

"Good shooting, Moses," Allen said. "All that practicing you did last year is paying off now."

"What do we do next?" Moses asked, pleased with the compliment about his shooting. "It'll soon be pitch-black."

"Well, we can't get back to the wagons tonight. We'd lose our way for certain. We had better stay here and save as much of this meat as possible. The wolves will think the prairie's turned into a dinner table if we leave it scattered like this."

They brought up the horses, staked them upwind, as close as they could get them to the dead animals without frightening them, and then made a bed between two of the dead cows. Working as fast as they could in the fading light, they butchered the other cows and carried the meat over close to their bed.

"This is certainly spooky country," Moses said as he munched on a piece of roast antelope and listened to the far-off howl of a wolf. "That wolf sounds as if he's planning to make a meal out of us. Don't you think we could start a small fire?"

"I'm more worried about Injuns than I am about wolves," Allen answered. "We can do without the fire. I don't think the wolves will come right up to us. If they do, a shot will drive them away."

Moses pulled his blankets up to his nose and tried his best to sleep. He thought that the night was terribly long, and that there must be a couple of hundred wolves moving closer to them each moment, judging by the howls. With each one, a shiver ran right up his spine. He wondered whether shivers were what made his hair feel as if it were standing on end. He hoped Allen couldn't sense that he was frightened. Well, it's not too bad, he told himself. He wasn't really scared. Not a bit. He could just think of a million places he would rather be than out here lying between two dead buffalo, listening to the wolves telling one another about all the food they smelled.

Exhausted, Moses finally fell asleep. He awakened suddenly to sounds of snarling, howling, and frantic neighing from the horses. He grabbed his rifle as he jumped to his feet, peering through the faint predawn light. The wolves were close! They were tearing at the pile of butchered meat. Then he saw a huge, shaggy, brown animal snarling as he tore at chunks of the precious meat. It was a bear! Saliva and blood dripped from his mouth. He reared up, facing Moses.

Moses aimed his rifle and fired. Bears could kill men and horses, too! With sharp fear, he realized that he had missed and hurriedly reloaded. Suddenly Allen was beside him. He fired and missed, too. Moses took careful aim, then saw that the bear, frightened by the shots, had dropped to his forepaws and started running toward the river.

Moses was so surprised that he lowered his rifle and watched the bear go. "Golly-whillikers! Am I glad that bear ran away from us and not straight at us," he said. "They sure do grow big out here in the mountains." The wolves, that were circling the dead cows, crept away as the sky brightened.

"You're right. I hope he's as scared of us as I am of him, and I don't mind saying so, either," Allen answered. He gathered some buffalo chips and lit a small fire. "Let's have buffalo tongue for breakfast. Then we had better finish the butchering and get back to camp."

Moses was so hungry that he was almost ready to eat the buffalo tongue raw. He led the horses down to the river and watered them while Allen prepared breakfast. "We should have brought some coffee with us, but the meat's good enough to make up for it," he said as he cut off a chunk of half-cooked tongue and shoved it into his mouth.

The two men worked hard at the butchering and were able to salvage most of the meat because the wolves and the bear hadn't done too much damage. They loaded the horses.

"It's late. Way past noon already," Allen announced as they began the trek back to the camp. "It'll be good to get back. I will admit that I prefer a tent and blankets to a bed between dead buffalo."

They walked for what seemed to Moses almost a hundred miles. When they stopped to rest for a few moments, he noticed that the sun was getting low.

"Shouldn't we be seeing the camp by now?" Moses asked, as he eased his boot back on his sore heel.

"Remember we rode most of the day yesterday. We're on foot now, and that makes a big difference. We'll soon be there. Don't worry."

"I'm not worried," Moses protested indignantly. "What do you think I am—a baby?"

"Calm down. You're as spiky as a porcupine. I'm a trifle uneasy myself because it looks as if we'll be out here another night." Allen stretched and yawned. "Do you think we should camp here for the night or keep going and try to find the wagons?"

"It's warmer walking," Moses answered in a tired voice. "I'd rather go on than wait for the wolves to catch up with us."

A few stars twinkled in the darkening sky, and the waning moon rose, but clouds scudded across its face, shutting out the small amount of light it supplied. They kept on walking, stumbling, leading the tired horses.

"At least we're bringing back plenty of meat, but I wish we would find the camp," Allen said after they had walked several more miles. "Those wolves are a long way off, but I don't like their howls."

"They're probably finishing the meat we left on the carcasses," Moses suggested hopefully. "Maybe that will keep them occupied for the rest of the night."

After walking another quarter of a mile, Moses turned and peered at the shadowy figure Allen made in the dim moonlight. "Say, Allen, are you sure we're not walking in circles? I think I've passed this same bush three times."

"All bushes look alike at night, Moses. I've been sighting by the North Star when I can see it, and we're going straight—in the right direction. We're keeping that range of low hills on our left."

"Yes, but we could miss the camp by a mile and go right past it."

"Sure we could, but as long as we don't cross the Sweetwater, we can't get lost."

They went on, stumbling over low rocks, pushing their way through bushes. Moses rubbed his dust-irritated eyes, and hoped they would find the camp soon.

He was hungry and tired, but he kept his spirits high by thinking about the meat. He had finally shot his share of buffalo, and he knew the company would need all that meat, and more, before the end of the journey. California was a long way off!

He smiled as he plodded on, pulling the reins of his tired horse. Maybe the amount of meat he and Allen had killed would stop some of the ribbing he had been taking. It would be nice when the men stopped talking about the great buffalo hunters who came back without buffalo or guns.

"Say, Allen, what day is it?" Moses asked suddenly. "Rather, what night is it?"

"Let's see. It's close to July, I think. No, it was July when we stopped. It must be around the third or fourth. I believe tomorrow's the Fourth of July."

"Golly-whillikers! The Fourth was a big day back in Missouri, and bigger yet in Ohio. In Ohio there was a mighty celebration and even a parade, and Elizabeth always fixed a special dinner with pie for dessert. Do you suppose we'll celebrate the Fourth way out here in the mountains?" Moses' voice sounded wistful.

"I think so," Allen answered. "But not with a parade, certainly. Too bad we can't have some games or a shooting contest, but I don't think the captain would stand for any wasted ammunition. He surely laid into us when we shot that old bull back on the Platte."

Allen laughed ruefully. "I imagine John Murphy will feel like celebrating the Fourth if he's back from the hunt."

"John? Why?"

"Didn't you know? That's one reason why we camped when we did. John's going to be an uncle again. Mrs. Miller should have had her baby by now."

"Golly-whillikers! No, I didn't. Think of that. A baby born way out here. That's really something!"

"You're right there. I wonder if any babies have been born on the Oregon Trail before."

"Maybe some were last year," Moses said, after reflecting for a moment. "Lots of folks started for Oregon last year."

"Yes, and some of them must have had a tough time, too. From what we've seen thrown away, they weren't very smart when they loaded up their wagons. Too much heavy stuff. Remember that monster of a cast-iron stove we saw back on the Platte?"

"Yeah. It sure looked funny sitting under that grove of cottonwoods. Mary Sullivan almost cried when she saw it. She said she's always dreamed of having a real stove." Moses peered at the sky. "Allen, don't you think it's getting lighter?"

"It seems to be. It must be almost morning. It'll be daybreak in a few more minutes."

At daybreak Allen and Moses saw the tracks of the

wagons. They were so exhausted that they almost went straight across them before they realized that the camp was off to their right.

"Hey! There they are." Moses' smile almost reached his ears. He walked faster, ignoring his sore heel. The herd guards were coming in, and the camp was waking as they trudged up to the wagons.

"Elizabeth," Moses called to his sister as she came out of the tent. "We brought back plenty of meat. Seven cows. How about that?"

She patted his arm. "That's wonderful. The other hunters came in last night. Their horses were loaded with meat, too." She laughed somewhat sheepishly. "I worried about you."

Moses moved away from her hand. "Aw, Sis! You can see I'm all right."

By this time the whole camp was stirring. The women were busy building fires and cooking breakfast. Moses' stomach rumbled with hunger. He grabbed a piece of bread and munched on it. Then he decided to find out how John had fared while he waited for breakfast and walked over to the Murphy wagon.

"Hey, John," he called. "How are you this morning? How many buffalo did you get?"

John rubbed his eyes. "Six, altogether. I shot two. We didn't get back until about ten last night. Say, what kept you so long?"

"Walking," Moses answered in a tired voice. "Just walking. All night long."

John smiled at Moses. "Did you hear the news? I'm an uncle. My sister had a baby yesterday. A little girl. They named her Ellen Independence after that rock and after Independence Day, too."

Moses turned and looked toward the great rock looming like a monstrous whale on the skyline. "I can't think of a better name," he said.

John nodded. "Guess I had better put away some breakfast. There's plenty of work ahead."

"Breakfast is just what I'm heading for now," Moses answered. "And hours and hours of sleep."

He slept until late in the afternoon when Elizabeth woke him, telling him that he would never sleep that night if he didn't get out of his blankets immediately. As far as he was concerned, Moses didn't believe he would have any trouble sleeping right through until the next morning, but he decided he had better do what Elizabeth wanted.

He was surprised by all the activity when he looked around the camp. Everyone was busy cutting meat into long, thin strips and hanging it to dry on racks made from the young cottonwood trees growing along the river.

"Mr. Greenwood told me how to make pemmican," Elizabeth told him. "There are quite a few berries growing near here, and they are almost ripe. After the meat is dried, I'll pound it and mix it with the berries and form it into cakes. He says that's the way the Indians do it, and that it keeps a long time, and is real filling."

"I'll help you," Moses offered. "We'll need plenty of meat before we get over the mountains to California."

↞ 8 ↠

AFTER spending a week laying up a supply of meat, the emigrants moved west along the bank of the Sweetwater River. They continued to send out hunting parties as long as there was a chance of getting buffalo. When the buffalo disappeared, there were still antelope and deer to shoot. Moses observed that Elizabeth made a practice of serving fresh meat, guarding the dried buffalo and pemmican as if it were raw gold.

The climb toward the summit of the Rockies was so gradual that sometimes Moses didn't believe they were climbing at all. He knew by the cold nights, thin air, and puffing oxen that they reached a higher elevation each day, but it was hard to realize how high they were until he found a thin sheet of ice on their water bucket one morning. Ice in July! He showed it to Elizabeth who told him she wished the ice would last until noon when a cold drink would be welcome.

When Mr. Greenwood announced that they had reached the summit, Moses couldn't believe his ears.

The old trapper must be mistaken. This simply couldn't be the summit of the great Rockies—the South Pass. Why, they had hardly climbed at all!

Moses followed Elizabeth and Dr. John to a small spring beside the trail. He stared unbelievingly and was forced to admit that Mr. Greenwood was right. The water trickled toward the setting sun.

"It just doesn't seem possible," Moses protested to his brother-in-law. "You think of the Continental Divide as something written with great big capital letters. Here it is—a little spring with a few drops of water trickling westward. And as for the South Pass—you would never know we were in a pass at all."

"I'll admit this pass isn't dangerous or awe-inspiring. You're looking for precipitous cliffs, craggy rocks, and a narrow trail winding precariously along the edge of a chasm. But think about it, Moses. If the only way through the mountains was a pass such as you visualize, we could never get wagons through it. The discovery of this pass by the trappers made the trail to Oregon possible. You had better hope that we can find as easy a route through the mountains between us and California." Dr. John lectured Moses as was his habit whenever he had an opportunity.

"I guess you're right. I realize a pass doesn't have to be dangerous, but the Continental Divide should be more than a little spring trickling out a few drops of water." Moses wasn't ready to give up.

"What did you expect? A full-blown river springing out of the side of a mountain and rushing full blast toward the Pacific Ocean?"

"No, I guess not, but there should be something more than this." With that Moses turned and went back to the wagons. He was disappointed, but happy. Reaching the pass meant that this journey was nearing the end. They must be more than half the way now, he thought hopefully, and they were certain to be safely over the California mountains before the snow fell.

Caleb Greenwood led the train down the banks of the Little and Big Sandy Rivers, heading toward the Green River. They camped on the bank of the Big Sandy an extra night because there was good grass, and because the cattle's feet, which had become sore from the rocky trail, needed rest. There Elizabeth had an idea.

"There's no reason why oxen shouldn't wear boots," she declared.

"That's foolish, Elizabeth." Moses and Dr. John spoke in unison.

"Oxen wouldn't take a step in boots," Dr. John continued. "What would you use for material, anyway?"

"I think they would, and there's plenty of material. All those buffalo hides we saved. You two stay right here. I'm going to ask Mr. Greenwood about it." With that she hurried off while Moses and Dr. John smiled at one another.

Elizabeth returned in a few moments with a triumphant smile on her face. "Old Mr. Greenwood knows every trick that helps on a journey like this. He had already told some of the families about boots for the oxen, and thought we knew about it. The Indians used to make boots for the feet of their horses when they were going to cross a desert or a rough, rocky place. He says it's an excellent idea because the country ahead is broken and rocky. So the two of you can stop smiling and sit right down and help me cut and sew the boots."

"Golly-whillikers, Sis! I was going hunting." Moses stalked toward the tent.

"You come right back here, Moses. I need you to cut the hides."

"Gee, Elizabeth, sewing is for women and girls. You can't expect a man to do it."

"Well, in the first place you're not really old enough to be considered a man yet, Moses Schallenberger. Besides that, men do these things more often than you think. Who do you suppose does the sewing for the mountain men that you follow around all the time? If Mr. Greenwood and Mr. Hitchcock hadn't done plenty of mending and sewing during the long months they've spent in the mountains their clothes would have fallen apart."

"All right. Don't nag. I'll do it, but I hope no one sees me with a needle in my hand."

"If anyone does, don't worry about it. If you'll look

around, you'll see Allen Montgomery and John Murphy both helping to make boots for their teams."

"All right. All right. Let's get it over with." Moses pulled out his knife and cut the hides, vowing that the next time they stopped for an extra day he would make himself scarce. "Women's work," he muttered under his breath.

After supper Moses wandered over to Mr. Greenwood's campfire, hoping to hear some more stories about the mountain men. He was nursing sore fingers, and he knew why Elizabeth cherished her thimble. Mr. Murphy, Mr. Hitchcock, and all the Greenwoods were there conferring quietly. Moses started to back away when Captain Stephens saw him and motioned him closer.

"Moses, go around the camp and tell the men we want to talk to them, and to the wives, too, if they want," he directed. "We're considering a change of plan, and they deserve a chance to talk about it."

Moses was so curious that his ears itched. He hurried around the camp with his message and then hustled back so he could hear what the leaders of the company were planning.

Captain Stephens addressed the travelers as soon as they had gathered around the fire. "As most of you know, Mr. Hitchcock has been west before. He claims there is a shortcut between here and the Green River that'll save us about a hundred miles. By the shortcut the

Green is only twenty-five miles away. That's just two days' march. The regular trail will take about eight days. I think we should take the shortcut. Every day we save means we'll reach the California mountains earlier and have a better chance of getting across them before the snow flies."

Dr. John listened intently. "What does Mr. Greenwood think about this idea? After all, we hired him to guide us."

Caleb Greenwood stood up and hooked his thumbs in the top of his pants. "Ain't got nothing agin it. I ain't been over this shortcut, but Hitchcock's a good mountain man and knows what he's talking about. I'm for it."

The men and women nodded agreement gladly as they realized they could save six precious days.

The company started as soon as the sky was bright, with Mr. Hitchcock leading the way. Moses soon discovered that the regular trail was almost as good as a Missouri road compared to this one, and that breaking a trail was both hazardous and tedious. He knew that there hadn't been too many wagons over the Oregon Trail before them, but the trail itself had been used by buffalo, Indians, trappers, and hunters for many years and was fairly well marked, winding around the rocks, following gentle grades over which wagons could easily pass.

The cutoff was different. Mr. Hitchcock knew where

he was going and led them without hesitation, but the ground was rough and rocky. There were no tracks to follow around the worst of the rocks and the roughest of the dips, and there was no water.

They went on, hour after hour. Moses thought they would surely reach the Green River soon. Then he realized he was being foolish because the oxen didn't travel faster than fourteen miles a day on a good trail. They probably weren't going half that fast over this rough ground.

As the sun grew higher, the cattle started to suffer from thirst. A few of the emigrants grumbled about the difficult route, but they were forced to continue on the shortcut. The shortest way now was forward to the Green River.

When the sun went down, Captain Stephens decided that they must stop for the night, even though they would have to make a dry camp. It was too dangerous to travel through such rough country in the dark. A broken axle or an injured ox would cost them precious time. Moses helped guard the restless, bawling cattle during the early evening, and at midnight crawled into bed. He rolled up in his blankets, hoping they would reach the Green River early the next morning. The cattle needed water desperately.

He was awakened suddenly by someone calling his name. He tumbled out of his blankets, rubbed his eyes, and hurried out of the wagon.

"You really do sleep! I've been yelling for five minutes." Daniel Murphy stood beside the wagon holding two horses.

"What's going on, and what are you doing with my horse?" Moses asked in a sleep-thickened voice.

"I'm saving you time. We're detailed to find out what happened to the cattle. You, Bill Higgins, Mr. Bean, Perry Derby, Mat Harbin, and me. Captain Stephens said so."

"Whose cattle?" Moses was still sleepy and didn't understand what Daniel was saying. "What happened?"

"Gee, you are a sound sleeper. The cattle that ran off during the night. Half the herd. Didn't you hear the commotion?"

Moses was becoming annoyed. "Well, they didn't run off during my watch. What's the matter with the rest of the guard? Can't they take care of things on their watch?"

"Who cares?" Daniel asked. "Going after the cattle ought to be more fun than slogging ahead with the oxen. Grab some breakfast and come on."

Moses took the plate of food that Elizabeth held out to him, thanked her, and was eating rapidly when the rest of the search party joined him. "Where do you think we should start looking?" he mumbled through a mouthful of flapjacks.

Mat Harbin spoke first, in a positive voice. "I think

we should go straight ahead to the Green. Cattle always head for the nearest water, and we're much closer to the Green than any other river."

"I don't agree with you," Mr. Bean said. "Cattle can't smell water that far, and they don't know there is water ahead of us because they've never been this way before. They went back to the Big Sandy."

Bill Higgins disagreed. "They wouldn't go back. Not through all that rough country. They're quenching their thirst waist-deep in the Green by now."

Daniel agreed with Mr. Bean. "I think they'd go back."

"You're no cattleman," Mat said. "Cows can smell water for miles. I just know they're on the Green. What do you think, Moses?"

"I think we're wasting time. The smart thing would be to divide into two parties. That way we'll have a double chance of finding them."

Mat Harbin nodded. The rest of the group agreed, and they mounted their horses. Moses, Daniel, and Mr. Bean headed back over the rough trail toward the Big Sandy.

It'll be a long, hot ride, Moses thought as he waved to Elizabeth. He decided he was lucky the cattle hadn't run away during his watch. Captain Stephens would have blamed him for it for certain after the cattle-stealing joke he and John had played back on the Missouri. They rode single file for several hours because of the difficult trail, spacing themselves about fifty feet apart to avoid the eye-irritating dust kicked up by the horses. Daniel Murphy took the lead.

Suddenly Moses saw Daniel throw up his arm, and then bend forward, flattening his body against the horse's neck. Moses pulled up as Daniel wheeled around, signaling for them to do the same.

Trusting that Daniel knew what he was doing and hadn't suddenly become sick from too much sun, Moses obediently wheeled his horse and started back toward a canyon they had just passed on the left. Daniel galloped behind them into the canyon and raced up it for a quarter of a mile. He pulled his horse to a halt and jumped from the saddle. Moses and Mr. Bean slid off the backs of their panting horses and waited for Daniel to explain his actions.

"Indians!" he whispered. He wiped his forehead and checked his pistols. "A hundred Indians, riding straight at us."

Moses whirled around and stared anxiously at the canyon's entrance. "They didn't follow us in here. Let's hope they didn't see us."

They stood quietly for several moments, scarcely daring to breathe, holding their hands on the horses' muzzles.

"Maybe we had better find out which way the Indians went," Daniel suggested.

"Why?" Moses asked, keeping his voice calm and

level. "We're evidently safe here. Why stick our heads out where they would be certain to spot us?"

"I don't mean that," Daniel said impatiently. "We can tie the horses here and crawl up the side of the canyon where we can see the Indians. They won't see us."

"This trip is something. Walking, riding, and now climbing," Moses answered in disgust. "All right, I'm game. I wouldn't want to ride out of here and head straight into a whole band of Indians, anyway. I'd hate to leave my scalp out here after all the way we've come." He thought a moment as he tied his horse to a scrubby tree. "Say, Daniel, what kind of Indians were they? Mr. Greenwood says the Snakes won't bother us."

"I don't know," Daniel answered. "I just saw Indians and didn't stop to ask them what tribe they belonged to or whether they were friendly or not. I thought the best thing in the world to do was move while I still had hair on my head."

"Well, that was smart," Mr. Bean agreed. "I don't think I would stick around and ask a bunch of Injuns which tribe they belonged to, either. Can't you see them laughing at the foolish palefaces while they sharpen their scalping knives?"

Once the horses were securely tied, the three men started climbing the steep side of the canyon. Moses was dripping with sweat before they were halfway to the top. This land was merciless, he decided. The sun's rays felt like rods of hot iron across his back. He knew there would be no respite from the heat until late afternoon.

They pulled their way to the top by grabbing at the small bushes growing between the rocks and by finding footholds on the rocks themselves. Moses moved cautiously, keeping a sharp lookout for rattlesnakes, praying that an inadvertent misstep wouldn't send the rocks tumbling down to the canyon floor and betray their presence to the Indians.

Moses panted as they neared the top. Slowly he raised his head just high enough to see over the canyon wall. Nothing but fifty yards of flat ground. Beside him, Daniel and Mr. Bean lifted their heads. Daniel motioned them forward, and they snaked across the fifty yards on their bellies and elbows, not daring to straighten up lest the Indians spot them on the skyline.

Before he reached the edge of the plateau, Moses heard the horses' hoofbeats. The rumble grew louder and he realized the Indians must be riding straight toward them. He moved forward another few feet and cautiously peered over the edge. Daniel had seen Indians all right! At least a hundred of them.

Moses caught his breath. They were Sioux! They rode closer, coming across the plain straight toward the three men. Moses' mouth went dry, his throat constricted, and he licked his lips as he saw the long bon-

nets of feathers and the symbol of war Caleb Greenwood had described on their painted faces.

He held his breath and flattened himself behind a
small bush as the Sioux rode nearer and nearer yet. He
could hear them talking. Suddenly he was desperately
afraid—afraid for himself, for Elizabeth, and for the
whole company. If the Sioux discovered three men
here, they would know a wagon train was nearby. He
closed his eyes and prayed that the Indians would pass
by without seeing them.

⤙ 9 ⤚

Moses barely breathed as he heard the Indians ride closer and closer. It seemed they must surely sense the presence of the men almost overhead. He buried his face in the dirt as the Indians rode by directly beneath them and prayed that their own horses would not betray them by nickering. The hoofbeats of the war party sounded like thunder in his ears, then gradually diminished.

Daniel was the first who dared to raise his head. He touched Moses on the arm and gestured that the Indians were going away. Moses turned his head sideways and stared at Daniel, a chill racing over him. Neither one dared say a word. Then Moses lifted his head a few inches and watched the Indians ride away with such a feeling of relief he felt almost sick.

They lay quietly for a few more moments. Then Mr. Bean broke the silence as the band of Indians faded into the distance. "I don't see how they missed us. Providence must be on our side," he said, shaking his head as he watched the war party disappear.

The three men crawled back to the other side of the plateau, not yet daring to stand for fear the Indians would look back and see them silhouetted against the sky. They scrambled and slid down the side of the canyon and ran to their mounts.

Moses untied the reins of his mare and gently rubbed her on the nose. "You beauty," he said. "You kept quiet." He turned to Mr. Bean and Daniel. "All the time the Indians were going by I kept wondering what would happen if the horses neighed."

"What if! What if!" Mr. Bean echoed impatiently. "If everything was ifs, we would never get to Oregon or to California, either. Life is what is, not what if. Right now our job is to find those missing cows. Come on."

They retraced their steps over the trail they had broken yesterday, back to the Big Sandy and discovered the cattle grazing peacefully on the bank of the river not far from where they had previously camped.

"Cattle remember the way back to water all right," Moses said. "I think these cattle could lead us all the way back to Missouri."

"They probably could," Daniel agreed, "but I wouldn't want to chase them any farther. Not with the Sioux roaming the countryside. Let's round them up. We have miles of riding ahead of us."

Mr. Bean looked thoughtfully at the sun, already

sliding toward the horizon. "It's pretty late to start back to the Green River, even though we won't be slowed up by the wagons. We can't make it before dark," he said. "Don't you two think we had better stay here for the night?"

"You're right," Moses answered. "If we start now we might stumble on those Indians in the dark. I would sure hate to see them again. They looked as if scalping was on their minds."

Daniel agreed, and they decided to stay in the old camp. As Moses unrolled his blankets and laid out some meat for supper, he decided that he was getting mighty tired of cold food. It seemed that he spent most of his time where a fire was dangerous. When I get to California, he promised himself, I'm going to get myself a house with a great big kitchen stove and stock plenty of food in the cupboards. And I'll keep the coffeepot hot on the stove from morning until night.

They took turns guarding the cattle during the night and started for the Green River at daybreak. The cattle went willingly, and Moses and Daniel found themselves singing as they ambled along behind the herd. Mr. Bean was riding in front, leading the way. Suddenly he galloped back, whipping his horse frantically.

He pointed to the top of a hill about a mile away. Moses swallowed hard as he saw two Indians sitting motionless on their horses, calmly watching them. Mr. Bean pulled his horse to a sliding stop beside Moses and Daniel and pointed ahead. "We're dead for certain!" he said.

Two more Indians on horseback drifted slowly onto the trail directly ahead of them and sat staring at the three men. Moses glanced back, wondering if they could escape by abandoning the cattle, and gasped. Indians were behind them, too.

"We're surrounded," he said in a hoarse whisper. "It must be the same band we saw yesterday. What shall we do?"

"They're going to charge," Daniel said as a band of Indians came over the skyline and started down the hill. "I'm for fighting," he added in a determined voice. "We might as well die like men as wait for them to take our scalps without doing anything about it."

"Me, too." Moses' face was pale. He set his jaw and raised his rifle. "I'll take that big one on the left, and I'll keep shooting at the ones on the left as fast as I can reload."

"I'll aim for the center," Mr. Bean said as he checked his supply of bullets. "After we've fired, don't wait to reload. Try to get through to the camp and tell them what's happened. Otherwise they'll be surprised like we are, and they'll all be killed."

"Not on your life!" Moses said flatly. "If we head for the wagons, we'll lead the Indians right to our people. I'm staying right here." It flashed through his mind that this might be the end of the journey for him, but he was grimly determined not to endanger Elizabeth.

"Me, too," Daniel declared. "We had better say good-bye."

Mr. Bean gulped. "I know you're right. I'll stay, too. Good luck to both of you."

Moses kept his eyes on the advancing Indians as they rushed down the side of the hill, yelling at the three men. His finger tightened on the trigger and his throat tightened at the same time. He thought again of Elizabeth and prayed silently that the Indians wouldn't discover the company.

Suddenly, before they came within rifle range, the war party stopped. Then three warriors rode slowly out of the middle of the band and came toward them.

"Guess they don't think we'll give them much trouble," Moses said bitterly as he aimed at the leading Indian. "We'll show them."

"Hold on!" Mr. Bean ordered, as the Indians moved cautiously to within two hundred yards. He threw up his rifle in a signal for the warriors to stop. They halted for a brief moment, then resumed their slow advance, watching closely for a sudden movement.

"They don't look like Sioux," Daniel said. "Not like the bunch we saw yesterday."

Moses was puzzled. "They don't act as if they meant to attack us." He pointed his rifle into the air and advanced warily to meet the Indians. Daniel and Mr. Bean followed him.

"They're not Sioux!" Mr. Bean shouted. "Glory be, we're safe!"

Moses wiped his sweaty hands on his pants and swallowed hard over the sudden lump in his throat. He had thought they were going to die, and he still couldn't quite believe that they weren't going to be tortured or scalped.

The Indians belonged to the Snake tribe. One aged warrior could speak some English, and he explained that they were searching for the party of Sioux warriors that had passed by yesterday. The Sioux were many miles inside Snake territory, and the Snakes were afraid they might come closer to their villages.

Daniel and Moses told them what had happened to the cattle, and the Indians volunteered to help drive the herd part of the way to the Green River while they hunted for signs of the Sioux. Late in the afternoon the Snakes left them, explaining that the Green was only a few miles away.

About an hour after sunset, Moses, Daniel, and Mr. Bean saw the dim outline of the wagons on the bank of the Green River.

"I'm starving. I hope Elizabeth saved me plenty of supper," Moses said to Daniel as they rode into the camp.

"Don't you ever think about anything but food, Moses?" Daniel asked with a laugh.

"Sure," Moses answered cheerfully. "Hot corn bread dripping with honey."

The wagons rolled on early in the morning. Mr. Greenwood was anxious to go as far as he could in one day after he heard about the war parties and the Snakes hunting for the Sioux.

"We don't want to get caught in the middle of an Injun war," he said in a worried voice. "I ain't blaming the Snakes none. If the Sioux get a toehold in their country, the Snakes might as well strike out for the Pacific Ocean. A Sioux never gives up, once he moves in. They fight like grizzly bears. Well, it ain't easy to beat them. I reckon the entire United States Army would have their hands full if they met up with a big band of Sioux on the warpath."

Caleb Greenwood and Mr. Hitchcock led them over rough, mountainous country toward the Bear River. The oxen and some of the horses were tired, red-eyed, and gaunt. They strained and panted as they went up and down the banks of small creeks. Dr. Townsend was worried about the condition of his horses and announced that he would attempt to do some more trading when they reached the Bear.

"Trading! Where are you going to find a place to trade out here?" Moses asked. Surely Dr. John wasn't considering riding up to a Sioux warrior and asking him to swap horses. He couldn't be thinking of trading with the Snakes. Their horses were so miserable and gaunt that their bones would poke holes in the saddle.

"Don't you ever listen to the plans for the next day?" Dr. John asked impatiently. "Greenwood says there's a trading post on the Bear River. It belongs to a man named Peg-leg Smith. He carries a good stock of horses and supplies. We don't need supplies because we laid in plenty of meat back on the Sweetwater, but I would like to exchange a couple of these horses for some that don't look as if they will collapse in another fifty miles. The pony I got for Elizabeth is in good condition, as is your mare, but the rest of our horses could go lame any day."

"Who is Peg-leg Smith, and why is he living out here?" Moses asked, wondering how anyone could survive so far from a settlement.

"Mr. Greenwood says he has a peg leg. He was wounded in the leg during a fight with the Indians. He amputated his own leg, knowing he would die if he didn't do it," Dr. John explained. "As to why he lives out here, maybe he just doesn't like civilization."

They reached the Bear River the following afternoon and camped close to Peg-leg Smith's trading post. Moses accompanied Dr. John to the combination cabin and store. The trader had few supplies, but he had a plentiful stock of furs for sale. Dr. John shook his head at the suggestion of beaver pelts and asked about horses. Peg-leg Smith claimed to have some spirited mares and led them out to the corral.

The trader was right. His horses were fat and lively. Dr. John was determined to have a couple to replace his worn-out horses. Allen Montgomery and Martin Murphy wanted to trade, too, because several of their horses were too exhausted to bear anyone's weight.

Moses watched the haggling, admiring the courage of the rotund trapper who had hacked off his own leg. He decided that these trappers were mighty shrewd. They seemed able to sense how badly their customers needed horses or supplies. Peg-leg Smith was just like the trader at Fort Laramie. He wanted all he could get and then a bit extra. Dr. John was forced to give two of the tired horses plus ten dollars for each fat pony he received in exchange.

"He sure comes out ahead on deals like this," Moses said as they led the horses back to the camp. "He'll fatten and rest our horses, and I suppose he'll trade two for one the next time, too. Good way to build up a fortune in horses."

"That's true, but if people like Peg-leg Smith weren't out here, we would have a tougher time getting to California," Allen answered.

"Actually, Moses," Dr. Townsend started lecturing again, "it's people like Peg-leg Smith, Caleb Greenwood, and old Mr. Hitchcock who make it possible for wagon trains to go through the mountains. Jim Bridger, who was a trapper, took the first wagon through the South Pass. If it weren't for men like him breaking the trail, and men like Hitchcock knowing about shortcuts, men like us would never dare attempt such a hazardous journey with our families."

"Mr. Hitchcock did save us time by knowing about the cutoff, even though we had to go back after the cattle, but the road was as rough as a hog's back," Moses agreed.

"Not only time for us, but for the people who will follow us next year and the year after that. They will all use Hitchcock's cutoff as soon as news of it reaches Fort Laramie."

The Bear River Valley was vivid green with tasseled grass. Elizabeth had gathered wild onions and picked berries to add variety to their supper. Moses and John Murphy tried their luck at fishing, but the mosquitoes, big and hungry, drove them back to the campfire.

They set out again the following morning with Mr. Greenwood guiding them down the trail toward Fort Hall. There were long discussions around the campfires every night, with many of the weary families talking about staying on the safe road to Oregon.

"How do you know you can get to California?" Mr. Bean asked skeptically. "As far as we know wagons have never even tried it."

"You know that's not true," Dr. Townsend answered.

"Chiles and Walker headed for California last year. We know they went through Fort Laramie."

"Well, you don't know that they ever got there. I'll bet they died crossing the desert," Mr. Bean argued.

"What about the mountains?" Mr. Derby asked. "You'll never get across those mountains."

"I started out for California, and that's where I'm going," Martin Murphy announced with grim determination. "There's a way over or through or around every mountain."

"You might get across the burning desert, but you'll be buried in the snow in those mountains. Nobody will even know you're coming, and they won't send help out if you don't get there. I'm going right on to Oregon. It's safer. Lots of folks got through last year. There aren't hardly any Americans in California, anyway. Just Injuns and Spanish," Mr. Bean added to bolster his argument.

"There are people in California," Mr. Hitchcock answered. "I know. I've been there, and that's where I'm going with my family. There's a wonderful fertile valley right over those mountains and lots of sun and no malaria. More Americans will come each year. Just wait and see."

Mr. Greenwood glanced at the solemn faces. "I'm for California," he announced. "Them that wants to can play it safe, but I ain't backing out now."

The arguments continued as the wagons neared Fort

Hall early in September. As far as Moses, Elizabeth, and Dr. John were concerned, there was no decision to make. They had started out to go to California, and to California they were going. It was the same with the Murphys and their relatives, the Millers and the Martins.

Fort Hall, glistening in the sun on the bank of the Snake River, was a joyous sight to the weary, travel-worn emigrants. Moses straightened in the saddle as they approached it and smiled happily at Elizabeth. They had made it all the way across the plains and over the Rockies to this fort—the last outpost.

He had heard much about this fort from Mr. Greenwood—that it had been built by Nat Wyeth and sold to the British who used it as a trading post.

"Thank goodness we started with plenty of flour and other supplies," Elizabeth said when Dr. John told her that the travelers who had run out of flour were paying a dollar a pound for it. Fortunately, everyone had an ample supply of dried buffalo meat from the hunt on the Sweetwater, in addition to the extra cattle that could be killed for food if the supply of buffalo wasn't sufficient for the rest of the journey.

Captain Stephens had selected a campsite near the fort, and they spent several days repairing the wagons and resting the oxen. Allen Montgomery accompanied the captain from wagon to wagon, inspecting axles, bolts, wheels, and chains. They made new tongues for several wagons, tightened bolts, and repaired the dusty, ragged canvas tops.

The captain reminded the emigrants that this was the last outpost. From here on, they would be on their own until they crossed the mountains and reached the fort John Sutter had built.

Moses grew tired of hearing the captain's warnings, tired of inspecting wagons bolt by bolt and piece by piece, tired of herding cattle, tired of the constant arguments about staying on the safe trail to Oregon. The three days at Fort Hall seemed like an eternity.

Captain Stephens, Dr. Townsend, and Martin Murphy tried to discover what had happened to Joe Walker and Joseph Chiles. They learned that the men had turned off the Oregon Trail for California the year before, but were unable to find out if they had reached Sutter's Fort. Captain Grant, the chief agent at Fort Hall, told them no word had come from New Helvetia, and no one knew what had happened to the Chiles-Walker party or their wagons. The tall, handsome captain pulled at his red whiskers and advised them against attempting the passage to California, telling them their bones would whiten in the desert.

Early in September the train of twelve wagons turned south from the Oregon Trail about two days' journey from Fort Hall. Mr. Bean, Mr. Derby, and the families that owned the other twenty-eight wagons decided against the unknown, dangerous trail to California and joined a company just behind them that was going to Oregon.

They had become very close during the long journey from Missouri. The dangers and hardships had drawn them together so that they were almost like one big family. When the twelve wagons turned south, Moses felt bereft, as if he were saying good-bye to his own kin. He would miss them all, Mr. Bean, Perry Derby, and even old Mr. Derby who had never once stopped criticizing the captain's orders.

Their twelve wagons made a mighty small train, Moses thought as he waved good-bye to the Oregon-bound travelers and then surveyed the unknown trail to the south. He straightened his shoulders and told himself not to be so gloomy. The road ahead was not completely unknown—not all the way. Trappers and hunters had been south as far as what they called the Sink—a place where the Humboldt River seemed to spread out and sink into the ground. A place that was the beginning of the desert.

Mr. Greenwood's contract had expired. He had been hired to pilot them only as far as Fort Hall, but he had elected to remain with the train and do his best to help them reach California. His familiar, buckskin-clad figure was at the head of the company.

They were a fairly well-organized group for a trek into the unknown, Moses had decided as he listened to the men discuss the route and plans. Mr. Hitchcock and Caleb Greenwood were certain that they could get through before winter. Although Mr. Hitchcock claimed to have been to California many years before, he couldn't remember the route, but was positive they would find an easy pass.

All the members of the Murphy family were optimistic about their chances. Dr. John and Allen Montgomery were determined and cheerful, too, and Moses felt better now that the final decision had been made; but he still wished that word had come back about the Chiles-Walker party.

The twelve wagons looked defenseless and lonely as they made their way south, heading into an unknown land, toward a burning desert and almost impassable mountains.

~ 10 ~

Moses realized it would be a dangerous and tedious journey from here on as the wagons rolled southwest beside a small stream Caleb Greenwood called Beaver Creek, explaining that the trappers used to bring out great piles of beaver pelts from this creek. Mr. Hitchcock said it was the Raft River but, whatever the name was, the trail beside it was difficult, over dusty country that had little vegetation. He knew that horses had been over this trail, but could find no traces of ruts made by Joe Chiles' wagons.

They were forced to make their own road now as they turned the wagons aside for large boulders and lowered them in and out of streams, sometimes stopping to dig down the steep banks.

They followed the bank of the Raft River for two days, grateful for a chance to camp close to water. Caleb Greenwood and Captain Stephens hurried them along, alternately tongue-lashing and encouraging the families that weren't ready to start on time or lagged behind during the day's march. Moses heard Captain Stephens remind the company that it was almost the middle of September so often that he suspected the captain mumbled the words in his sleep.

Elizabeth asked Francis Deland to put a regular saddle on her horse the morning they left the Raft River. She mounted and pulled her full linsey-woolsey skirt down as far as possible.

"I'm sure glad I learned to ride astride," she said as she rode beside Moses. "A sidesaddle is all right, but not for all day. My feet are sore from walking, and I know I couldn't stand to ride in the wagon."

"You'd be jolted to pieces in an hour," Moses answered, studying the rock formations in the valley they were entering. Huge granite boulders were scattered across the arid land. Great blocks of rock of all shapes and sizes lined the sides of the valley. "It looks as if a giant had been playing marbles with the rocks," Moses said thoughtfully.

"Playing marbles, indeed!" Elizabeth answered. "There's nothing playful about this land. It's frightening and desolate. I feel dwarfed and deserted. The rocks remind me of a terrible city where people have been forbidden to live."

Mr. Greenwood led them around the Goose Creek Mountains. When they reached a steep descent, the company stopped and locked the wagon wheels, then lowered the wagons into the valley by ropes.

They followed Goose Creek, and about two weeks after leaving the Oregon Trail came to a small stream which Mr. Greenwood told them was the headwaters of the Humboldt River. They camped for the night. Dozens of Indians drifted into camp as soon as they stopped. Moses was told that they were called Diggers, and promptly hunted up Mr. Greenwood to find out why these Indians had such a peculiar name.

"They dig roots for vittles," the guide explained. "They appear friendly enough," he added somewhat dubiously. By this time scores of Indians were roaming through the small camp, looking longingly at the cooking pots and peering into the wagons. "We'd better keep a right smart eye on our belongings. These Injuns are poor. If they see blankets or rifles lying around loose, they ain't apt to pass them by."

Moses watched the guide attempting to talk with the Indians and realized from his gestures that he was asking the way to the land beyond the mountains, as he pointed southwest. Mr. Greenwood didn't know the language of the Diggers, and it was obvious the Diggers didn't speak any dialect except their own and a few words of Snake. They didn't understand Caleb Greenwood's sign language and shook their heads at his gestures.

The wagons rolled easily along the bank of the Humboldt. It took them three interminably long, monotonous weeks—weeks of freezing cold nights and incredibly hot days—to reach the Sink where the river disappeared into the desert.

Moses had complained about the tedious journey and the bitter-tasting water, but he realized they were fortunate. Grass was plentiful along the three-hundred-mile stretch following the Humboldt, and the oxen and horses were in good shape, despite the distance they had traveled.

Moses' spirits lifted as he heard Caleb Greenwood and Captain Stephens tell the company it would be a good idea to remain at the Sink a few days to rest the oxen, even though they were sound and hardy. He helped pitch the tent, and then carried water as Elizabeth began the usual routine of washing and cooking.

The water was extremely brackish, and coffee made with it was so unpalatable that Moses grimaced at the first mouthful, then forced himself to drink the rest in the cup, realizing plain water would be worse.

A strict guard was set around the camp at night because great numbers of Indians continued to visit them. Moses took his turn on the first watch, then rolled up in his blankets, tired but happy. He had shot two ducks during the late afternoon. He planned to hunt in the morning and hoped he would get a deer. As he drifted off to sleep he told himself that this wasn't such a bad place. It was a strange place—with the river spreading out into bogs and pools. A swamp was the last thing he had expected to find in this arid country. Even though the water was foul-tasting, there was plenty of game. Best of all, the long journey was almost finished. They would be in California soon.

The next morning Martin Murphy raced up to Captain Stephens. "I told you not to let those Indians have free run of the camp," he complained. "One of my horses was stolen last night. A good, fat pony that I traded for at Peg-leg Smith's. Come on! I want him back."

Captain Stephens turned to Mr. Greenwood for advice. "What do you think?"

"We would be crazy as loons if we made one hostile move at these Injuns. Hundreds of them would swarm all over the camp if we did. One pony ain't much to lose if they leave us alone. Besides, I warned everyone to keep close watch."

"You're right," Captain Stephens agreed. "But we had better double the herd guard. The loss of more horses would put us in a pickle."

Moses was coming back to the camp after shooting two sage hens and overheard the discussion. He wondered at the captain's caution. The Diggers had no weapons except bows and arrows so it should be easy to keep them away from the camp. He shrugged and carried the game to Elizabeth. After breakfast, he helped Allen Montgomery tighten bolts and grease their wagons, then took his turn at herding cattle.

The captain called the entire company together that

evening and asked for suggestions. "We must decide which direction to take from here," he told them.

"Doesn't Mr. Greenwood have a route in mind?" Allen Montgomery asked.

"Nope," Caleb Greenwood answered tersely.

"How about the Indians?" Martin Murphy suggested. "They should know the way to California."

"Maybe so," Mr. Greenwood answered. "But they're a stupid bunch—too stupid to understand Snake or Crow. They just stand there like old cows when I ask them. A sadder bunch of Injuns I ain't never seen. Don't smile, don't laugh, don't know nothing."

"I wonder which way the wagons went last year," Dr. John said quietly. "It's queer we haven't observed anything we could be certain were wagon tracks."

"If they came this way, their tracks might have been erased by the winter," Captain Stephens answered. He rubbed his head thoughtfully and appraised the small group, stretching out his neck so that he resembled a turkey more than ever. "It's past time to make up our minds and head west," he continued. "We can't afford to waste time. Winter's coming fast."

"I think we should go south and hunt for a gap in the mountains," Dr. John said.

"How do you know we'll find a gap? Maybe there's nothing but desert for hundreds of miles," Martin Murphy objected.

They argued for several hours, with some saying

south and some saying west until Moses decided they would never come to an agreement. Finally the men went to bed without making a decision. The argument continued the next day and the next, with both men and women straining their eyes, looking south and west, trying to pierce the hazy air to see what lay ahead of them. Moses wished they would stop arguing and get started. They would surely find a pass if they went west.

Caleb Greenwood spent hours each day patiently trying to communicate with the Indians. One morning he hurried into the circle of wagons with an old Indian in tow.

This one is different, Moses decided, staring at the Indian who smiled and laughed as Mr. Greenwood gestured to him.

"He resembles an old French trapper we used to know in Canada," John Murphy said.

"He sure does," Daniel agreed. "What was his name?"

"They called him Truckee," James Miller said.

"Well, that's a good name for this Indian," Moses suggested. "Let's call him Truckee. I wonder what Mr. Greenwood's doing with him?"

"Why are we standing back here? Let's get closer and find out," John said.

They walked over to watch Caleb Greenwood who was so excited he was almost jigging up and down.

"Get the captain!" he shouted to Moses. "I finally found me an Injun with some sense in his head."

Moses hurried off to find the captain. The rest of the company, attracted by the shouts, gathered around the Indian who nodded sagely at the guide's sign language.

Truckee and Mr. Greenwood squatted on the ground facing each other. The Indian smoothed the dirt between them and picked up a small stick. Captain Stephens' face brightened as Truckee started scratching on the smooth ground.

"Golly-whillikers! That looks like a map," Moses said, almost shouting with excitement. He bit his lip as Captain Stephens turned and glared at him, wondering if he would ever learn to keep quiet.

"It sure does," John Murphy said in a low voice. "Maybe he knows the way to California."

Caleb Greenwood studied the scratches for several long moments and then straightened up. "Yep, a sensible Injun! This is the route to take," he announced with a broad smile.

"What route?" Dr. John asked. "What does he mean?"

"Looky here at his signs. He's saying there's a river about fifty or sixty miles west of us. The river flows east out of the mountains, and there's good grass and large trees along the stream. It ain't no trouble to get through there."

"How can you be so positive?" Martin Murphy asked as he looked doubtfully at the Indian.

"It's sure as sunrise. That's the way to get through mountains. Follow the rivers. Like we did the Sweetwater. Rivers don't skitter over the top; they come down through the mountains."

"Are you positive that this Indian knows what he's talking about, and that he understands what you want to know?" Dr. Townsend asked. "I'm not going to subject my wife or wagon to a trip of fifty or sixty miles across that desert out there just on the strength of a few scratches made by an old Indian."

"Got a better idea?" Captain Stephens asked curtly.

Dr. John shook his head.

The captain studied the faces of the men and women gathered around him. "Well, we can't sit around here much longer. Dr. Townsend's right about this Injun, though. We had better take a look for ourselves and make certain he didn't conjure up the river. Dr. Townsend, Joseph Foster, Caleb Greenwood, and I will ride out with the Injun to guide us and find out if there's a river."

Dr. John started away to get his horse. Moses raced after him while Elizabeth hurried to pack some provisions. "Can't I come, too?" Moses asked. "There's nothing to do here."

"No, you can't! You stay here and take care of

Elizabeth." With that Dr. John saddled his horse and hurried to join the exploring party.

Moses and John Murphy stood beside the wagons watching the explorers ride off into the desert.

"We're old enough to watch the herd at night, but have to stay put here with all these women and kids and Indians. I don't see why they couldn't have let us go along, too," Moses grumbled.

"You might as well stop complaining. There's nothing to do except wait until they come back."

"How long do you think it'll take them?"

"Fifty or sixty miles is what Mr. Greenwood said." John thought for a moment. "Well, they certainly won't be back tomorrow. Probably not until late the next day."

The men were gone three days. Moses hunted every morning and did his usual chores, complaining about the acrid water and the gnats and flies.

He walked about a quarter of a mile from the camp with Elizabeth late in the afternoon of the third day. Her face was pale and drawn. She clutched his arm tensely as she looked southwest for a sign of the exploring party.

"They should be back by now," she said anxiously. "They must be out of food. Whatever will I do if something's happened to Dr. Townsend?"

"Don't worry so. They are all right." Moses took off

his jacket and spread it out on the ground for Elizabeth. "Let's sit down," he suggested. "We'll see them soon."

Elizabeth sat on the jacket, tying and untying the strings of her bonnet as she stared at the desert.

Moses peered across the arid countryside, shielding his eyes from the sun. "Look!" he yelled. "There they are! That cloud of dust."

Elizabeth jumped to her feet and wiped her eyes. "I'm so glad I could cry," she said watching the riders coming closer to the camp. "We mustn't let Dr. Townsend know we were worried about him. Let's hurry back so I can start supper. He'll be hungry."

Captain Stephens wore one of the few smiles Moses had ever seen on his face as he led the party into the camp. "The river's there, all right. Nearer than Truckee said it was. About forty miles away. Get ready, all of you. We'll pull out tomorrow."

Dennis Martin seemed doubtful. So did Ollivier Magnent.

Captain Stephens gave them a long, hard stare. "Anyone who doesn't want to start can stay here and die alone!" he roared. "I'm leaving as soon as the sun rises. It's almost the middle of October. If we stay here any longer, we'll get caught in the snow. I'm not going to freeze to death!" Captain Stephens' voice dropped on the final words to a low, serious tone. He swung around, walked swiftly to his wagon, and started checking supplies.

"We'll all be with you, Captain," Martin Murphy called after him. He turned to the worried emigrants. "Captain Stephens and Dr. Townsend have seen the river. It's out there! It's not a figment of some Indian's imagination or a misinterpretation of the map. We must leave here now. We'll have trouble with both the Indians and the weather if we don't, and I want you young men to calm down about the Indians. Maybe, as John Greenwood claims, they have stolen some of the oxen, but we've gotten them back. The oxen probably strayed in the first place. Anyway, hold on to your tempers and get ready to leave."

Dr. John gave Martin Murphy a look of approval. "It'll take two days to reach the river," he said. "All of you should prepare extra supplies and fill everything you can with water. You'll need it." He beckoned to Moses and they started filling tubs with the brackish water while Elizabeth cooked extra rations.

As they ate supper, Dr. John pointed west, across the desert. "You'll like the river, Elizabeth. It tastes like nectar compared to this water, and from then on the journey will be easy. It's no more than a hop, skip, and jump to California."

Elizabeth leaned against his arm. "It sounds as if you were describing a paradise. I'll be glad to leave here. The Indians make me nervous." She stood up to clear away the dishes, then abruptly turned back to Dr. John. "Is that old Indian you call Truckee going to guide us?"

"No need for that. We know the way." Dr. John grasped her hand and pulled her down beside him. "Let's sit here for a time and enjoy the fire."

Moses took his turn at the first watch. When he was relieved, he hurried to the wagon and drew his blankets over him. He closed his eyes with the thought that they would be in California in just a few days.

In the morning Moses jumped out of bed early. He pulled his clothes on and hurried outside to saddle his horse. He reached for the halter he had left hanging on the side of the wagon. It was gone. He turned to Elizabeth who was bending over the fire.

"Did you see my halter?" he asked.

She shook her head.

Moses turned and walked around the wagon. No halter. He knew he had left it hanging on the wagon. He searched the ground close by and still couldn't find it. He returned to the fire wondering where it could be. Standing near Elizabeth was a Digger wearing a short feather blanket. Moses stiffened as he looked at the young Indian.

"Give that to me!" he shouted. "That's my halter!"

The Digger stared at him impassively.

"That's my halter under your blanket!" Moses shouted in a voice that could be heard all over the camp. He pointed to the halter, then to the wagon, and then to himself. "You stole it!"

The Indian ignored Moses as if he could see the sky

through his body. Then he stepped back, behind the fire.

"That's mine!" Moses raced forward and grabbed the end of the halter. The Digger jerked away, raising his bow.

"Why, you thieving rascal! Shoot me, will you! Steal my halter!" Moses' voice rose to a roar. He ran to the wagon, grabbed his rifle, and turned, aiming at the Indian.

"Moses, stop it!" Elizabeth screamed.

"What on earth are you doing?" Martin Murphy rushed up and pulled the rifle away from Moses. "You'll get us all killed."

Men and women ran up from all sides. Indians poured into camp from every direction, surrounding Moses and the young Digger who held tight to the halter. Mr. Greenwood fought his way through the crowd to the center of the group where Moses stared angrily at the Indian who was talking excitedly to his companions.

"That's my halter!" Moses protested.

Mr. Greenwood shoved Moses away. "You're a dad-blamed idiot!" he exclaimed and turned back to the irate Diggers, holding up his empty hands as he attempted to calm them. "Get me something for presents. Anything! Quick!" he ordered.

Elizabeth reached for the meat she was heating for breakfast and handed it to Mr. Greenwood. Blankets and more food were given to the Diggers who then quieted down and backed out of the camp. The young thief strutted triumphantly as he held the halter high in the air.

Dr. Townsend glared at Moses. "Have you lost your wits? Don't ever do a thing like that again! Those Indians could have wiped us off the face of the earth without any trouble. If you don't control your temper, you'll get us all killed. Now get another halter and get your horse ready. We're leaving."

Moses' face burned like fire as he raced to obey Dr. John.

⚬⊰ 11 ⊱⚭

THE FIRST wagon had already pulled away from the Sink. As the others followed, clouds of fine alkali dust, penetrating and choking, filled the air. The dust crept into Moses' ears and nose and coated his tongue and lips. Rivulets of sweat rolled down his face, making fine, maplike lines on the frosting of dust.

He rode, with head and shoulders drooping, close to his own wagon for a short distance. He knew that Elizabeth was still angry with him. She spoke to him only when he asked a question, answering in a clipped, cold voice. Finally, discouraged and remorseful, he dropped back to the Sullivans' wagon, wondering if Mary would speak to him.

"This is sure miserable country," he said tentatively.

Mary Sullivan tightened the strings of her bonnet and wiped her dust-covered lips. "I hope the river Truckee found for us is clean and good-tasting. That Humboldt! The clothes I washed in it smell as if they had been scrubbed with stinkweed."

Moses slowed his horse to match the pace of the Sullivans' oxen. "I meant to ask how long they figured it would take us to reach the river. I had guard duty last night and didn't hear what the captain said."

"He said we'll keep going until we get there. There's a spring about halfway. He said the water's boiling hot and won't be good for the cattle. There's no other water at all. We filled our buckets and kettles with that horrible water from the Sink."

"Same here." Moses smiled wryly, remembering how many bucketfuls he had lugged to the wagon. It seemed like enough for an army. "Elizabeth's had me carrying water during most of this journey. If it isn't water to wash clothes in, it's water to drink."

The company moved at a steady pace throughout the morning. They stopped briefly at noon and fed the animals grass they had cut at the Sink, then pushed on westward across the desert.

Moses watched gratefully as the sun slid down behind the wall of mountains looming in the west. Maybe the dust wouldn't be so sticky and itchy once the air was cooler. He slogged on, leading his horse, trying to breathe lightly as he coughed and choked.

He tried to clear his dry, irritated throat, but spitting and hawking made his mouth and throat burn. He rinsed his mouth with a sip of water and moved away from the wagons.

The sky darkened rapidly as they kept on across the desert, stumbling, choking, grimly moving ahead as the shadows lengthened. Captain Stephens rode up and down the line of wagons, encouraging the women. "Keep going!" he shouted. "It's easier on the cattle to travel at night." He lashed out at the men who lagged behind. "Keep them rolling!" he yelled. "Move those teams!"

Moses took his turn driving the oxen. Knee-deep dust swirled around him. It clogged his nose and mouth and he pulled his neckerchief up to just below his eyes. He couldn't draw a deep breath. He set his teeth and concentrated his attention on the plodding teams. He had to keep them moving!

Elizabeth swung down from the wagon and handed him some cold meat. Moses thanked her and bit into it. The meat tasted of alkali and was frosted with dust. He forced down a small piece and a swallow of water. He felt tired, discouraged, and sorry for himself until he looked at the oxen. They had been without food or water for over fourteen hours, but still plodded ahead pulling the heavy wagons through dust and sand that sapped their strength with every yard.

About midnight Captain Stephens rode back and announced they were nearing the spring where they would rest for a few hours.

As soon as they stopped at the spring, the dust settled. Moses gratefully took deep breaths of fresh air, wiped his dust-caked face and neck, and poured dipper after dipper of water over his head. Then he drank deeply, not even noticing the alkaline taste he had complained of so bitterly back at the Sink. Refreshed, he walked over to the spring. Steam rose from its surface, swirled upward, and disappeared into the cold night air.

"Couldn't we cool some of the water in tubs for the oxen?" Moses suggested to Dr. John. "They are so thirsty it hurts me to look at them."

Dr. John nodded his approval.

They filled a tub and sat leaning against a wagon wheel waiting for the water to cool. Moses marveled at the stillness of the night and the clear, clean sky in which the stars shone brilliantly now that the dust had settled. Elizabeth had crawled inside the wagon and gone to sleep the minute they stopped. Except for the panting, pawing cattle, everything was still. Moses thought that the day's terrible trek was almost like a bad dream—that he would wake up safe and comfortable in Missouri.

They sat quietly for a few moments. Moses leaned his head against a spoke of the wheel and almost drifted off to sleep. When Dr. John moved, he shook his head groggily and stood up to help water the animals. They took the lead team to the tub, and the animals sucked greedily at the water. Moses smiled as he watched them. Suddenly the oxen lifted their heads, snorted, and started to heave.

"Pull them away!" Dr. John shouted. "The water's bad." He threw the tub on its side.

Moses hunched his shoulders as he went to get another team. Nothing he suggested was right. Now two of the oxen were sick, and it was his fault. He helped chain the team to the wagon, and they started off again, driving the sick oxen with the herd.

The hours went by slowly, painfully, as they pushed on across the punishing desert. Finally the sky paled, and the sun rose behind them. The air grew hotter and hotter as the sun hammered its rays on their heads. Dust swirled around them. The oxen panted, snorted, and bawled for water. Moses staggered forward, doggedly putting one foot in front of the other, yelling at the team, smiling grimly at Elizabeth when he saw her worried face.

"We'll make it!" he shouted. "Don't worry. Just keep inside the wagon, in the shade." Moses coughed and choked as he yelled at the oxen. He wiped sweat from his dirt-crusted face and blinked tears from red-rimmed eyes. Would they ever get through this terrible place? Maybe they would all perish here in this never-ending inferno of heat and dust.

Noon came. The men pushed on grimly, cracking their whips across the backs of the teams, knowing that they would die if they stopped. Early in the afternoon Captain Stephens sent back word that they were approaching the river. The tired oxen moved ahead ponderously, then almost imperceptibly increased their pace.

Elizabeth screamed as the wagon suddenly jolted from side to side.

"Unhitch the teams!" Captain Stephens shouted desperately. "Cut them loose. They smell water. We'll lose everything!"

Elizabeth jumped from the wagon and watched as Dr. John and Moses hurriedly unyoked the teams. The herd was out of control, stampeding as the cattle smelled the water. The oxen galloped after them as soon as they were free.

"That was close," Dr. John said. "We would have lost the wagon in another few minutes."

"Come on, you two," Moses suggested eagerly. "Let's ride ahead to the river and get a drink. My mouth's drier than all the deserts in Africa, and our horses must be mighty thirsty."

Elizabeth unhitched her horse from the back of the wagon as Dr. John swung into the saddle. They rode toward a thin, green line, barely visible through the dust thrown up by the stampeding cattle.

"Look! Trees! It seems as if I haven't seen a tree in years," Elizabeth said. "I wonder what this river is called."

"It doesn't have a name," Moses answered with a laugh, happy that his sister was speaking to him again, so relieved they were across the desert that he felt like turning cartwheels.

"What do you mean, it hasn't a name? All rivers have names." Elizabeth was indignant.

"Not this one." Moses laughed again. "When no one's seen a river before, it doesn't have a name. As far as we know no one's seen this river except maybe that old Indian we called Truckee."

"Then it's his river and ought to be named after him." Elizabeth rode in silence for a few yards. "If we are the first people to see it except old Truckee, we can name it, can't we?" she asked.

"You name it, Elizabeth," Dr. John suggested, smiling tenderly at her.

"Then let's call the river Truckee. The Indian deserves to have the river named after him for having told us about it." Elizabeth looked ahead at the cottonwood trees and grass growing along the banks. "It's a lovely place. The prettiest place I've seen in months and months."

By the time the exhausted travelers reached the river, the thirsty cattle were knee-deep in the water, sucking and blowing.

"They'll drink themselves to death!" Dr. Townsend shouted. The men waded into the river and drove the cattle out. They guarded them carefully, permitting them to drink only small amounts at a time.

As soon as they were able to bring up the wagons and establish a camp, Captain Stephens and Mr. Greenwood conferred with the rest of the men, and they decided to remain at the river for two days.

"A dry pull saps the strength of a team," Captain Stephens explained. "No sense in pushing the oxen beyond endurance."

"The people need a rest, too," Dr. Townsend added, glancing around at the weary, dust-caked women and children. "What everyone needs right now is food and sleep."

"And baths," Elizabeth added.

Moses groaned. "Golly-whillikers! We reach a river that should be alive with fish, and the first thing you think of is a bath."

✑ 12 ⌁

Two DAYS later they left the camp on the Truckee River, high-spirited and optimistic. The oxen were rested and well fed. The travelers had scrubbed the clinging dust from themselves and their clothes and blankets. They had slept and cooked an extra supply of food, and now they started into the mountains—the last obstacle between them and California—with cheerful faces and determined steps.

Moses believed that they could do anything after crossing a desert like the one they had just come through without losing a single animal. Dr. John's lead team had recovered from the effects of the spring water and was pulling the wagon again. His heart beat faster as Moses studied the mountains. Beyond them lay California, and the end of the journey.

Even though they were breaking a trail, the way was easy. The wagons rolled smoothly along the bank of the Truckee River, and there was plenty of wood for fires, grass for the cattle, and game to shoot for food. Although it was mid-October, and the nights were chilly, the days were pleasantly warm as the sun continued to shine in a cloudless sky. They pushed on rapidly, following the stream into the wall-like mountains, and made good progress for the first few days.

John and Ellen Murphy, Elizabeth, and Moses were riding just ahead of the wagons the third day out. "It seems as if these hills get closer together all the time," John said somewhat apprehensively. "There's not much riverbank now."

"It's the river that's going to cause trouble," Moses said. "Look at the turns it makes ahead." He pulled his horse around with a twist of his wrist. "I'm going back to the wagons. Everyone will need to help if we are to get through that crooked stretch."

They worked together, easing the wagons into the water and hauling them out on the other side, only to be forced to cross the river again after moving along the bank a short distance. At nightfall Moses discovered that they had crossed the river ten times that day and made only one mile.

"If we could only rest for a few days," Elizabeth said as she huddled close to their fire.

Dr. John shook his head and pointed to the light snow whitening the peaks of the mountains. "We dare not take the chance. But we'll soon be over the summit," he added encouragingly.

The next day Captain Stephens and Mr. Greenwood rode up and down the line of wagons, urging the tiring travelers to push on as fast as they could. The oxen moved more slowly each time they were driven into the river. Their hoofs were softened by the water and worn down by the stones in the stream's bed. The boots Elizabeth had made for them ripped on the rocks, providing no protection for their sore hoofs.

"Each day of this is worse," Elizabeth said, dispiritedly. "Everyone is so tired."

"Not just the people. The oxen, too," Moses answered.

"I know it. I've never heard anything as pitiful as the way those poor animals are bawling," Elizabeth said, covering her ears for a moment. "Sometimes I feel like crying with them. Can't we stop and give them a chance to rest?"

"You know better than that." Moses smiled encouragingly at his sister. "The oxen can stand it, and so can we. We have to go on as fast as we can. If we get caught up here in the snow, we're likely to die. All of us. Both Captain Stephens and Mr. Greenwood said so."

Looking at his sister's distressed face as she turned away, Moses was sorry he had been so frank. Then he shrugged. The women had to realize they couldn't afford to waste a single hour.

The next day was worse, and the following one a

nightmare of endless crossings. Finally the wagons had to move directly in the riverbed because there wasn't room to pull them along the bank.

Moses watched their teams anxiously. The oxen's feet were so sore from the sharp rocks in the stream that they bawled with each step. He jumped from his horse and waded beside the animals, coaxing them along.

After half an hour the oxen stopped. Moses, Francis, and Dr. John shouted and cracked their whips over the backs of the teams. The oxen bawled and snorted, moving their huge heads from side to side, but refused to take a step.

"Get those wagons moving!" Captain Stephens yelled.

"The oxen won't budge!" Moses shouted back.

"You're holding up three wagons. Get them started!" Captain Stephens' voice was hoarse from constant urging, coaxing, and shouting. He sat on his horse and watched as they tried, without success, to get the oxen to move. The tired animals stubbornly refused to take a single step. "Add another team," the captain ordered, "and crack that whip harder. We must keep moving!"

They yoked four more oxen and chained them to the Townsends' wagon. Dr. John yelled and cracked his whip. The oxen lowered their heads and pulled the creaking wagon slowly up the stream.

When they stopped for the night, there wasn't

room to pitch the tents on the bank—just enough space to get the cattle and wagons out of the icy water.

Moses and Dr. John gathered wood and started building a fire. Elizabeth glanced at them, as she pulled supplies out of the wagon, and shook her head. "You two have no sense at all. Go change those clothes," she ordered. "You'll be sick if you don't get those dripping pants off right now, and I don't see why I always have to tell you to put on dry clothes."

"We'll be sicker if we don't get a fire built so we can get warm," Dr. John answered. "Just give us a minute."

The fire flickered and flared after they shaved some twigs onto the first flames. Moses added several larger logs, sat down close to the welcome heat, and looked around him. The mountains towered over him, making him feel small and insignificant. He shivered and moved closer to the fire as the wind whipped through the gorge. This was not a bad campsite, he thought, forcing himself to be cheerful. There was grass for the cattle, and now that they were out of the water, the oxen had stopped their incessant bawling.

Elizabeth dumped dried meat into a heavy, black kettle and mixed it into stew for supper. She threaded chunks of bread on forks and held them over the fire until they turned golden brown. Moses' nose twitched as the aroma of stew and toast filled the air. He stood up and crawled into the wagon to put on dry clothes and a pair of moccasins.

When he came out, the meal was ready. Elizabeth announced that this was the last of the bread she had baked during the two-day camp. "Enjoy it," she said. "I don't know when I'll have a chance to bake again."

"Your flapjacks are better than bread," Moses said cheerfully as he took the plate she handed him and sat down close to the fire. His feet were raw and blistered from walking in the water, but he refused to complain, knowing how the poor oxen, forced to plod through icy water on bruised, battered hoofs, must feel.

He ate rapidly and stretched out on the ground, staring up at the sky. Wisps of clouds scurried across the stars. Moses shivered and pulled his jacket across his chest.

"Do you really think we'll make it?" he asked Dr. John in a low voice. He didn't want Elizabeth to hear him.

"Of course, we will. We mustn't get discouraged now. We'll soon be in California, and we'll make a fortune selling the goods in the wagon. Then I'm going to buy Elizabeth a big California ranchero." Dr. John's optimism was apparent in his steady voice.

Moses glanced at the sky again. The clouds were thicker, heavy-looking, coalescing into a sodden gray mass. "Those clouds seem mighty bad," he said. "What will we do if it starts to snow?"

"It won't snow much. It's too early in the year." Dr. Townsend's voice was flat, almost daring the clouds to drop a single flake. "But if it does, we'll just keep moving. The snow won't be deep. Maybe a couple of feet or so, but it'll melt right off. There's nothing to worry about."

Moses shook his head, but decided he had better not argue. Dr. John was mighty positive and arguing just made him more certain that he was right. Moses stood up, walked over to the wagon, climbed inside, and slipped off his moccasins. Still in his pants and shirt, he pulled his blankets up to his ears and pillowed his head in the crook of his elbow. After shivering for a few moments, he fell asleep.

He woke up so stiff and cold that he pulled the blankets over his nose and curled into a tight ball. It was too early to get up, he decided, because the light filtering into the wagon was gray. His feet felt like stubs encased in ice and he rubbed them against the rough blankets, but he couldn't get warm. He heard the crackle of a fire and smelled coffee. It must be morning, but where was the sun?

He slung a blanket around his shoulders, moved to the back of the wagon, pushed the canvas covering aside, and stared out with dismay as a flake of snow hit his face. The ground was white and snow clung to the branches of the trees.

"Golly-whillikers, Elizabeth! Dr. John!" Moses shouted, waking them both. "It snowed! And it's still snowing."

He pulled on his still damp boots, grabbed his jacket, and swung off the tailgate, sinking almost to his knees in wet, clinging snow. He brushed it away from the site of the fire, looked across to the next wagon and waved to Allen who was already drinking coffee, then he pushed the old ashes and some twigs together. The twigs were so wet that the fire wouldn't burn until he reached under the wagon, pulled out a handful of dried grass, and carefully fed it to the flickering flames. He added the smallest twigs slowly and then a larger chunk of wood.

Dr. John helped Elizabeth down from the wagon. She wrapped her shawl tightly around her shoulders and reached for the coffeepot.

"Help get the teams ready, Moses. I'll watch this fire," Elizabeth said in a subdued voice. She shivered as she studied the whitened mountains and snow-laden trees and brushed snowflakes from her face. "Captain Stephens will hurry us off this morning the moment he comes out of his wagon."

Moses and Francis yoked the oxen before gulping down their breakfast. As Elizabeth had predicted, Captain Stephens took one look at the snow and shouted that he wanted the wagons ready to roll in another five minutes.

Moses mounted his horse and rode out ahead of the wagons to see what the day's journey would be like, thankful that the snow had stopped falling. As far as he could see the river was just as crooked—like a snake coiled in the mountains. He realized that another brutal day of slogging through icy water faced them, and went back to help with the cattle. The teams balked at the first crossing and bawled as the stones cut into their sore feet. Moses winced as he saw them whipped and goaded—forced by the drivers into the bed of the stream. By midmorning the men were walking in the water beside the oxen, and they had trebled the teams. They shouted at the animals, cracking the whips across their backs, forcing them to drag the wagons upstream as the river curved tortuously to the right and to the left.

Captain Stephens rode back and forth, from one end of the company to the other. He seemed to be everywhere at once, throwing his weight behind a wheel stuck against a rock, shouting at the drivers, pushing them relentlessly as the morning brightened and the sun gleamed dimly through a thin layer of clouds. "Eat whatever you have left, but keep moving. We won't stop this noon," he said as he went past the Townsends' wagon.

Elizabeth handed strips of buffalo jerky to Moses, Dr. John, and Francis. Moses sat on a boulder at the edge of the river munching on the meat. Dark, ominous clouds filled the sky to the west. He shivered as he chewed the stringy meat, and then he looked ahead and shivered again at the thought of getting back into the water. His feet were soaking wet from wading beside the oxen, and so cold they were numb. He wondered how much more the teams could stand as an ox slipped, bellowed, and staggered, leaning into the yoke. Moses winced in sympathy as the tired animal bellowed again, straining to keep up with his teammate.

The oxen were so gaunt it seemed as if their bones would rub through their hides. Moses realized that the animals were almost at the end of their strength. Even his dependable mare was showing the effects of the journey. She was thinner than he liked; her coat was dull. He bit his lip and clenched his fist as he looked at the mountainsides curving like scimitars down to the river. He straightened his shoulders and strode back into the icy water. They had to get through!

They made camp on the bank of the river when the light faded and the heavy shadow of the mountains darkened the narrow gorge. Moses helped unyoke the teams and moved them to the side of the wagon. They bawled for food and pawed at the snow. Moses patted the lead oxen on the head.

"Poor thing!" he said. "I'd help you if I could, but all the grass is covered with snow, and it's too deep to dig down."

When Elizabeth handed him his share of the scanty evening meal, Moses pushed the meat back and forth on his plate and stared into the fire.

"What's the matter with you? Why aren't you hungry?" Elizabeth demanded.

Moses shook his head. "I'm hungry all right, but I just can't eat and listen to those oxen bawl for food. They're starving."

Elizabeth laid down her fork. "Poor beasts. Feet so sore that each step must be like walking on knives. Now nothing to eat."

"Maybe they would eat pine needles," Moses suggested. "There are plenty of pine trees around."

"Let's try it!" Elizabeth jumped to her feet and ran to the nearest tree and shook off the snow. Moses pulled out his knife and started cutting the ends of the branches.

Each carried an armload back to the oxen. "Here, fellows," Moses said. "This isn't grass, but it might make you feel better."

The oxen refused to touch the branches. Elizabeth coaxed them, patting their heads, but couldn't get the animals to eat any of the needles.

When they went to bed, the oxen were still bawling. Moses couldn't get warm and slept fitfully with the blankets over his ears. As long as he was awake he heard the oxen, and he heard them still bawling the first thing in the morning. Elizabeth twisted and pulled up her blankets.

"Are you awake?" Moses whispered.

"Yes. I've been awake most of the night. Those poor

animals. They bawled all night long. Isn't there something we can do?"

"Not a thing. Not until the snow melts or we get through these mountains," Moses answered quietly so he wouldn't disturb Dr. John. "The sooner the better, so I'll get up and start the fire."

"I'm coming, too," Elizabeth said. "I can't lie here listening to this a moment longer."

When Moses saw Elizabeth's face in the gray light of the cloudy morning, he wondered whether she was wearing out from the long journey. She was pale. Her eyes were smudged with sootlike circles, and she moved slowly.

"Are you feeling all right?" he asked, helping her down from the wagon.

"I'm fine. Just tired. But so is everyone."

They broke camp early that morning and the next, moving sluggishly, determinedly, up the canyon—the oxen bawling with each step. All of the spare oxen were in use as the wagons were dragged forward by trebled teams. Moses and Dr. John watched Elizabeth anxiously and did their best to spare her. She looked as fragile as a candle flame. She wanted to help lead the oxen, but Dr. John ordered her to stay on her horse. "I don't want you to get wet," he said, concern making his voice brusque.

John Murphy rode back from the head of the train

and shouted at them. "Mr. Greenwood has found some rushes up ahead sticking out of the snow. He thinks the oxen will eat them."

When they reached the rushes, they saw the cattle ahead of them tearing at the plants like wolves at a buffalo carcass. They unyoked their teams and led them over to a tall clump of rushes. The starved animals ripped the rushes from the ground. Saliva rolled from their mouths as they shredded the plants.

"Watch those cattle!" Dr. John ordered. "They're so famished they won't know when to stop. They can eat themselves to death."

Moses and Francis stayed by the animals, pulling them away when Dr. John decided they had eaten enough. Moses walked over to the fire Elizabeth had started, sat down, pulled off his wet boots, and stretched his legs toward the welcome heat.

"Things look better now, don't they?" he said to John Murphy who flopped down beside him.

"They sure do. If the cattle leave any rushes standing, we can cut them and take them with us tomorrow," John said. "I'm not going to worry any longer. Mr. Greenwood always knows what to do."

"Maybe it won't snow any more," Moses said optimistically. "This snow is melting. Soon there'll be grass for the oxen again." He rubbed his feet and put on the battered boots. "I had better get some water for Elizabeth." He stood up, reached for the bucket, and then jerked around, staring at the other side of the camp. Excited voices rose high in the still air, and the men ran back and forth. "What's happening now?" he asked.

John jumped up. "Let's go see."

"The cattle are dying! My cattle are dying!" James Murphy rushed up to them. "Do something! Where's Dr. Townsend?"

Dr. John leaped out of the wagon. He raced across the camp to James Murphy's two foundering oxen and shook his head sadly as he looked at them. "I told everyone not to let the cattle gorge themselves. They've eaten too much. There's nothing I can do."

"Pull them away from the rushes!" Captain Stephens ordered. "Then finish your suppers and get to bed. We'll start early tomorrow."

It was barely daylight when Captain Stephens shouted the order that started the company moving. He directed Moses and John Murphy to ride ahead and search for rushes.

Moses grinned at John as they rode upstream, happy that he would have a few hours away from the laborious task of driving the teams. John's shoulders were hunched. He rode like a tired, old man.

"Golly-whillikers! Your chin's almost touching the ground. What's the matter?" Moses asked.

"I'm worried," John answered. "I heard the captain

and Mr. Greenwood talking about the oxen. They said unless we found more rushes the oxen would soon die of starvation. That we would have to leave the wagons and push ahead on foot."

"What a worrier you are! We'll find plenty of rushes." Moses led the way upstream around the first bend and the next. When they had gone two miles, Moses pointed ahead and turned to John with a teasing smile.

"See that clump of rushes. It's big enough for to-night and tomorrow, too, and it looks like a good place to stop. I don't think the wagons can get any farther today. Do you?"

John shook his head. He looked up the stream, leaning from his horse to see around a bend. "Let's go on. The river looks different around that bend, but I can't quite see what happens."

They went on, around the bend. The river was just the same, narrow and crooked. They decided to ride ahead for another mile. The sky was bright blue, and the sun warmed their shoulders. Melting snow slid from the branches of the pines with a soft rustle. Even though the air was piercingly cold, Moses felt tinglingly alive as his horse trotted along the bank. They rounded another bend after half an hour of riding, pulled up their horses, and stared at each other with troubled faces.

The river forked. The main stream came from the

southwest. A smaller tributary tumbled in from almost due west.

Moses studied the two rivers, pushed back his hat, and turned to John in dismay. "What do we do now? Which is the right way to go?"

◁ 13 ▷

Moses and John rode silently back to the wagons and told Captain Stephens about the division of the river a few miles ahead. The company reached the fork early the following afternoon, camping first at the stand of rushes. Because there was plenty of space beside the river for a campsite with stretches of yellowing grass where the snow had melted, Captain Stephens decided they would stop even though several hours of daylight remained.

After supper the captain called a meeting of the company. "We must decide which way to go," he said. "Any ideas?"

The tired travelers were slumped against wagon wheels, fallen logs, and boulders. Their strained faces were gray with fatigue. Some sat with bowed heads; others stared impassively at the captain. No one spoke.

Martin Murphy stirred impatiently. "We must make

a decision," he said. He grasped the spoke of a wheel and pulled himself to his feet. "We can't stay here. Every hour we waste increases the danger from the weather."

No one answered. The men sat hunched, discouraged, staring into the blazing fire. Martin Murphy turned to Caleb Greenwood. "What do you think?"

"Ain't saying," Caleb Greenwood answered. "Appears like one way would be as good as the other."

"Well, Captain Stephens, what do you suggest?" Martin Murphy asked.

The captain rubbed his hand along his jaw. "We could toss a coin." He shrugged. "The tributary appears easiest for the wagons."

"Maybe the best plan is to try both ways," Dr. Townsend suggested quietly.

Martin Murphy swung around to face Dr. Townsend. "What do you mean by that?"

"Either way should get us through the mountains. We could split up and try both. Then the first party to reach Sutter's Fort could send back help."

"That's a right smart idea." Captain Stephens nodded decisively. "We can send a party on horses up the main stream. The rest of us can take the wagons up the tributary." He stopped to think for a few moments. "We had best send fast horses and good riders up the stream so they can whip through in a hurry. We're mighty low on supplies."

Dr. Townsend nodded. "Elizabeth's a good rider and has a surefooted horse. How about sending your daughter Ellen?" he asked Martin Murphy. "Francis can go along to give the women a hand with the camp chores and make it easier."

"Ellen rides well," Martin Murphy agreed. "John and Daniel should go, too, I think." He looked gravely at Dr. Townsend and then nodded.

Caleb Greenwood scratched his head. "Sounds right sensible to me, especially since it's the middle of November and the weather's apt to close in on us. But they ain't experienced. Magnent had better go along. He's a good man. They'll need pack horses, too."

Moses listened to the discussion, wishing he was going with the horseback party. He didn't say a word because he knew he would be needed with the wagons, especially since Dr. John had already decreed that Francis Deland should go to help Elizabeth.

His sister motioned to Moses as she stood up and shook out her skirt. "Come and help me pack the supplies so we can start early tomorrow," she said.

They walked back to their wagon. Elizabeth opened the supply box. "It's almost empty," she said. "Francis and I won't need much food because we will move faster than the wagons. And we can hunt game." Elizabeth took Moses' hand in both of hers. "I don't like the idea of separating. We've come this far together, and I think we should stay together. I'll worry about you and Dr. Townsend." She moved closer to Moses and put her arms around him, holding him tight. "Promise me one thing, Moses," she said in a muffled voice, her face against his chest. "I want you to take good care of Dr. Townsend and of yourself and the wagon, too. We'll need the goods when we get over the mountains and down into the California valley."

Moses nodded. His throat was too tight to speak. He knew that Dr. John was right in sending Elizabeth ahead. She rode as if she were part of her horse. She would get to Sutter's Fort long before the wagons could reach the valley, and she would be safe. He wondered briefly if Dr. John was doubtful about the company's chances and had grasped at the opportunity to get Elizabeth out of danger. He told himself sternly not to be so pessimistic. Of course they would all get through.

Shortly after daybreak Moses watched the small party ride toward the southwest. Elizabeth was soon hidden in the mists that rose from the water, and he swallowed hard as she vanished from sight. What if he never saw his sister again? With a deep sigh he turned to the job of coaxing the tired teams to pull the wagons up the smaller river.

At nightfall they came to a little lake nestled high in the mountains. Moses caught his breath in dismay as he looked west. A craggy mountain mass thrust upward a thousand feet at the end of the lake. "Golly-whilli-kers," he said to himself. "Wagons can't go up there. Neither can women or children. It's an impassable barrier!"

They made camp and built up the fires. The men scouted ahead, hoping to find a route through the mountains before the twilight faded. Moses took over Elizabeth's duties and prepared supper.

When Dr. John returned with the exploring party he shook his head at Moses' anxious question about a pass. "We'll find a pass tomorrow," he said, "but I think we had better leave our wagon here."

Moses was thunderstruck. "Leave the wagon! Not when we've brought it this far," he protested.

Allen Montgomery studied the mountains towering above them. "I think you're right, John," he said slowly. "My oxen are too worn-out to drag a wagon up those cliffs. I'm not going to freeze to death for the sake of what's in the wagon."

"Do we have to decide right now?" Moses asked. "Maybe tomorrow someone will find an easy pass and everything will be all right."

"Don't be too hopeful," Dr. John said, getting up and

poking at the fire. "All we saw this evening was a stiff climb."

The men searched for a pass all the next day. They returned to the camp exhausted and alarmed. There was no easy way over these mountains. By evening Caleb Greenwood decided they would have to take the wagons straight up the steep slope at the western end of the lake.

"That settles it!" Dr. John announced. "We'll go on horseback. Our wagon stays here."

"Mine, too," Allen Montgomery said.

Caleb Greenwood and Martin Murphy moved closer to hear what was being decided. "Ain't heard a better idea in weeks," Mr. Greenwood said. "Been thinking the same thing myself. The wagons will still be here in the spring. We can come back and bring them out then."

"I thought—" Moses started to speak and then stopped, wondering if his suggestion would be laughed at, if he would be criticized again for interrupting.

"What, Moses?"

"I thought we needed the things in the wagon so we could get a good start in California."

"That's true," Dr. John said. "We need the tools, and the things we brought to sell so we can buy land, but Mr. Greenwood's right. We can come back for them."

"Maybe we should leave all the wagons," Captain

Stephens suggested. "We have enough horses for every-one."

"Not mine!" Martin Murphy, Jr. objected. "My wife's too close to giving birth to ride a horse. She would never make it. Besides, we need the wagons to carry provisions and for shelter for the children."

"That's true," Dr. John agreed. "No one can trans-port three or four children on a horse."

"That ain't impossible, either," Caleb Greenwood drawled. "But I reckon we can get a few of the wagons through."

"Have you found a pass?" Moses asked with hope and excitement in his voice.

"Nope," the trapper said slowly, "and it ain't going to be easy. We'll empty the wagons and lug the sup-plies ourselves. Not so much strain on the teams that way."

Captain Stephens yawned and straightened his thin shoulders. "We'll start the first thing in the morning. It will take a day to get around the lake. Right now I'm heading for my blankets. It'll be a tough day tomor-row."

"They've all been tough," Martin junior answered as he turned toward his wagon.

In the morning Moses rolled out of his blankets early and started cooking breakfast. He saw that the sky was filled with threatening clouds. The cold air bit into his bones, and he huddled close to the fire. He could hardly wait for Dr. John to come out of the tent. He had wanted to talk with him about the wagon last night, but when the other men started discussing the pass and the difficult ascent, he had decided to wait until they were alone.

Dr. John stretched and rubbed his eyes as he came up to the fire. Moses poured his coffee and held out the cup.

"I have an idea," Moses said. "Could I? Well, maybe I could—"

"Could you what?"

"I'll stay with the wagons." Moses blurted out the words.

Dr. John reached out and patted Moses on the shoulder. "That's a generous offer, but I can't let you do it. It's out of the question."

"Give it some thought, John, before you make up your mind." Allen sat down beside them. "It's a good idea. There must be Indians somewhere around here. They might loot the wagons. We need our tools and furnishings, and we'll need the money we'll get from selling the silks and satins in the wagons. I'll stay, too. You can watch out for my wife until you return for the wagons."

"But there's no bread or flour left, and not much meat. You'll starve."

Moses realized that there was a chance Dr. John would agree to his plan. "There's plenty of ammunition," he argued. "We can kill game for food. It won't be dangerous. There's bound to be lots of game here, and there's not much snow now."

Allen Montgomery leaned forward eagerly. "You know, John, we'll have some mighty poor years if we don't save the stuff in our wagons. The snow probably won't get any deeper than it is now, and the Indians must have already gone south. They won't bother us this winter. But if they should come back in the spring before you get here, we'll guard the wagons."

Dr. Townsend sat still for a short time, staring at his hands. "I don't know what Elizabeth would say if I left you here," he said to Moses. "I can't stay with you. I have to get to Sutter's Fort to take care of her." He looked from one to the other, unable to make up his mind. "I'll talk to Captain Stephens and see what he thinks. It's a good idea, but I'm afraid it's too dangerous."

Moses busied himself washing the breakfast dishes. He looked carefully at the wagon wheels and axles and asked Allen if he thought they were still all right.

"Sure they are. I've checked every time we stopped."

Joseph Foster came up to them. "What's this I hear

about you two planning to stay behind with the wagons?"

"We don't know yet if we can. Dr. John went to talk to Captain Stephens." Moses dumped water on the fire.

"I heard them talking. The captain said it was all right with him. I told them I would stay, too. I might as well since I was planning to leave my wagon behind anyway. My oxen are nothing but bones."

Allen clapped Joseph on the shoulder. "That's great," he said. "We'll build a cabin near the lake. With three of us to work on it, we'll have it finished in a couple of days."

"We're starting in five minutes." Dr. John and Captain Stephens walked up to the group. "Are you three absolutely certain you want to stay here?" Captain Stephens asked.

Moses answered for all of them. "We're positive. We'll be fine here until you get back."

"We'll leave you two cows. They won't go another mile anyway," Captain Stephens said in his usual laconic manner. "I'm leaving my wagon." He turned away and then turned back, looked keenly at Moses and gave his hand a quick, firm shake.

"Wait a minute," Caleb Greenwood said. "These three ain't staying behind yet. We'll need all the men we got to get the wagons up the first stretch. It's a pull that'll take our arms out at the socket."

Moses looked at Joseph and Allen, shrugged, and reached for his saddle. "That's fine with me."

"You three can walk back from the summit," Captain Stephens said. "We'll need all the horses to get down to the valley."

⌒ 14 ⌒

ELIZABETH's thoughts turned back to her husband and brother as the small party rode along the bank of the Truckee River. She disliked leaving them, but she realized that dividing forces gave them all a better chance to reach California. John, Daniel, and Ellen Murphy were excellent riders. Ollivier and Francis were competent hunters and would keep them supplied with game. She knew she would have no trouble with her horse. John had certainly been shrewd when he got this Indian pony at Fort Laramie. He was surefooted and intelligent, the best horse she had ever ridden. She was confident that they would get through all right, but she still wished the whole party had remained together.

Ellen Murphy rode up beside Elizabeth. "You seem worried. What's the matter?" she asked.

"I just don't like the idea of separating. What if we

never see any of them again? We might never know what happened to them."

"Don't say that! We'll get through to Sutter's Fort in a few days, and we'll send help back."

"I know we'll get through, but the more I think about it, the more worried I am about the rest of the company." Elizabeth's voice was low and grave. "I suspect Dr. Townsend sent me ahead because he was afraid they were going to have trouble with the wagons."

"Cheer up. This should be fun. I'm tired of riding beside those poky wagons." Ellen smiled and urged her horse ahead to join John and Daniel.

They followed the river, moving easily along the bank, until they came to a huge lake surrounded by pine-covered hills. The deep blue water sparkled in the sunlight. Elizabeth pulled her cloak around her shoulders as she looked at it. "I would have given almost anything to have seen water like this a couple of weeks ago, but right now I'm too cold to appreciate it," she said.

"Let's cross the river and camp for the night on the other side," John suggested. "We'll have to cross anyway and head west. We might as well do it now so we can dry out."

Elizabeth guided her pony into the water and discovered that he was an excellent swimmer. Glancing back, she saw that Ellen was having trouble. Her mare balked at the water's edge. Ellen kicked her hard and forced her into the water. John, who was a few feet in front of Ellen, waited until she was beside him then grabbed the halter and pulled her horse across the river.

There was plenty of wood, so the men built a blazing fire on the bank. They stood close to the flames as they ate supper. Elizabeth was still shivering when she rolled herself in her blankets for the night, and she alternated between periods of wakefulness and light sleep. She was so glad when it was finally daylight that she started the fire before the rest of the party awoke.

After a scanty breakfast, they skirted the edge of the lake, following the west bank for some distance, and then stopped to rest.

"As soon as we come to any kind of water flowing away from the lake, we'll follow it," Ollivier said. "Eventually we'll come to a big stream that we can follow down into the valley."

They camped the second night on the banks of a small, swift creek. Elizabeth rinsed her hands in the water. She gasped, jerked her fingers out, and stuck them in her mouth.

"That's funny. My fingers feel as if they were scalded." She stood up, shaking her hands.

"That water is almost ice," Ollivier said. "You had better keep your hands out of it."

John went hunting and came back with two rabbits

which they skinned, dressed, and roasted over a small fire.

"Isn't it queer how easily a person can get used to eating charred, half-cooked game?" Ellen asked as she tore into a piece of rabbit. "We used to have fruit compotes and trifle and biscuits. Here we are, miles from nowhere, sitting around a campfire eating with our fingers, and the food tastes better than a savory."

"I would prefer a chunk of buffalo tongue," John said. "This little bit of scrawny rabbit isn't filling. I could eat six of them."

"What I really want is a slice of crusty bread hot from the fire with yellow, fresh-churned butter and strawberry jam on it, and a tall glass of cold milk," Elizabeth announced in a dreamy voice.

"Don't talk about things like that," Daniel said. "I can't even remember how a good meal tastes or a bed feels." He stretched, and unrolled his blankets.

They started at sunrise, following the creek toward the west, even though the water drained into the lake. They realized that they would have to cross the divide before they would find a river running westward. Elizabeth was dismayed as the creek rapidly narrowed. Late that afternoon they reached its source, high in the mountains, and camped beside the trickle of water.

"Now what?" Ellen asked.

"We head west. Straight west. We should be over the summit soon," John answered cheerfully.

All the next day they rode west, climbing, threading their way over the mountains. Several days later they came to a swift river that descended rapidly between high hills.

"This is worse than the Truckee," Ellen said, shaking water from her skirt after fording the river for the third time. "The rivers in these western mountains curve like scallops on a dress. It seems as if they want to flow backwards."

"That current is dangerous," John said. "Be careful, Ellen. Your horse worries me. She hates water worse than a cat does."

They stopped at the edge of the stream after picking their way slowly along the narrow bank for several hours. It was impossible to continue without crossing because a ten-foot-high ledge rose straight from the edge of the water.

"We'll have to ford here, and then again at that bend down there," Elizabeth said, pointing downstream. "I have an idea. John, you and I can cross first. Then you can take my horse back for Ellen."

"That will slow us up an awful lot," John objected.

"So it will, but there's no point in drowning."

They forded the river five times that day, with Elizabeth's pony doing double duty at each crossing, and finally decided to stop for the night.

"At least we're out of the snow, and it's somewhat

warmer." Elizabeth revolved in front of the fire, trying to dry out her soggy skirt.

"Maybe John will find more game now that the snow is gone. Something bigger than a rabbit." Ellen searched through her saddlebag and then through the packs that Francis had taken from the extra horses. "I thought I could find some morsels of food, but there isn't a single bite left."

"You can stop hunting for crumbs in those packs." John swung down from his horse and smiled at Ellen. "Here's a real dinner." He pulled the carcass of a small calf from behind his saddle.

"Wherever did you get that?" Ellen asked, staring at him in dismay.

"There are lots of cattle roaming about. We must be getting close to a ranch." John avoided Ellen's accusing eyes.

"But that calf belongs to someone! You had no right to kill it."

"I know that," John said impatiently, "but I didn't see any other game. Neither did Francis or Ollivier, and we're hungry."

"But, John, we can't go around killing cattle that belong to other people." Ellen's cheeks flushed bright red and her eyes snapped. "You know what Dad would say. He's always told us never to take anything belonging to anyone else."

"I know it! You don't have to tell me!" John glared at Ellen and then started roasting the meat. "If you feel that way about it, you don't have to eat any. I'll be glad to have your share."

Ellen sniffed and tossed her head as she watched the juices roll down the joint John had suspended over the fire. When the meat was ready, she ate her serving with her eyes lowered, refusing to look at him.

"Tastes good, doesn't it?" he teased. "What happened to your scruples, Ellen?"

Elizabeth patted Ellen's arm. "Stop teasing her, John," she said. "You know as well as Ellen does that this isn't right, but there's nothing else to do."

The river was still swift and crooked the next day, and they made many crossings, using Elizabeth's pony twice each time. Late in the afternoon John rode the pony back to get the pack horses after helping Ellen across the stream.

"Pretty tired, aren't you, fellow?" John patted the horse and coaxed him into the water. The pony faltered halfway across the stream on the return trip and slipped on a rock. He swam a few yards, then regained his footing, struggling against the current.

"Come on, boy. You can do it!" John leaned forward, talking in soothing tones. Suddenly the pony fell. John shouted as he was thrown into the water. The vicious current caught him and swept him downstream, out of sight.

"Help him!" Elizabeth screamed.

Ollivier and Daniel spurred their horses and raced down the bank.

Ellen sobbed as she jumped into the saddle. She slapped her reins and kicked the mare into a run. Elizabeth followed right behind her.

"There he is!" Daniel yelled as they rounded a bend. John was wedged against a low-hanging willow, with one arm caught in the branches, his head back and his eyes closed. The current knocked him against the rocky bank. Daniel and Ollivier pulled him from the water, and Ellen unrolled her blankets and wrapped them around his limp body.

"He's breathing, but he's terribly cold. Get a fire started. Hurry!" she ordered in a shaking voice.

John moaned and opened his eyes. "I guess we should have stopped a bit earlier," he said weakly. "Did anyone get the horses?"

"Are you all right, John?" Ellen asked, rubbing his hands.

"Of course I'm all right." John pulled away and struggled to sit up by grabbing at a low branch. "Someone get the horses!"

The pony and the pack horses had reached the bank a few yards below them and stood shivering at the water's edge. Elizabeth told Francis to take care of them as she piled more wood on the fire.

"This is as good a place as any to camp," she announced. She turned to John. "You were lucky to land against that tree."

"I didn't land. I grabbed for the branch," John said. "I thought I was gone for sure."

"So did I." Ellen had tears in her eyes.

"Don't cry. I'm all right now. Let's have something to eat and then get some rest," John suggested. He pressed Ellen's hand for a moment, then moved first one leg and then the other, wincing as he tried to stand.

Elizabeth looked at him anxiously. "Lie still," she ordered. "You've had a bad banging around, and you'll have to ride again tomorrow."

The river straightened out the next day, and the way was easier as they continued along the bank. John and Daniel killed calves for food, and Ellen scolded them each night for doing it. John was weak and tired from the banging he had taken in the water, and all of them were becoming exhausted from many days of riding. No one wanted to leave the river's edge to hunt game, so they killed the calves when they needed meat.

Late one afternoon, about three weeks after they had left the wagons, Ellen pulled her horse to a stop and pointed down the valley. "I'm almost afraid to say it, but I think I see something that looks like a house," she announced in a trembling voice.

Elizabeth peered in the direction Ellen pointed. "It *is* a house!" She swung around in the saddle. "Look, everyone!" she shouted. "We made it! We made it!"

They forced the tired horses into a trot and then a canter as they neared the house.

"We don't look very presentable to go calling," Elizabeth said. Her smile was bright as the sun.

"Who cares?" Ellen grinned. "Let's hope we're near Sutter's Fort, and that we can get there soon."

They rode up to the house, shouting and laughing with relief and excitement as a man and woman came out to meet them.

"I'm John Sinclair," the man said. "This is my wife. Where in the world did you people come from?"

"For goodness' sakes, John," Mrs. Sinclair interrupted. "Can't you see that these people are cold and tired? Don't stand there asking questions." She hustled them inside the house and started heating food and coffee after pushing Ellen and Elizabeth into chairs.

"Are we near Sutter's Fort?" Elizabeth asked. She leaned back, somewhat dazed. She hadn't realized how exhausted she was from the long days on horseback and from worry about Moses and Dr. John who were constantly in her thoughts.

"Just a few miles northeast of it," Mr. Sinclair answered. "But who are you? Where did you come from?"

"We're the Murphys," John answered. "This is Mrs. Townsend and Ollivier Magnent and Francis Deland. We came from Missouri."

"Just you? On horseback? How on earth did you do it?"

"No, not just us. Our families. With wagons," John explained.

"Wagons! Where are they?"

"We must get to Sutter's Fort right away," Elizabeth said urgently, moving toward the door. "My husband and my brother are up in the mountains with the wagons and the rest of the company, too. We must send help and supplies back so they can get through."

Mrs. Sinclair gently pushed her back into the chair. "You can't go on tonight, so you might as well sit down and get warm. You need some food, too." She bustled to the fireplace and put more wood in it. "Supper will be hot in a moment."

Elizabeth leaned back in the chair, then stood up and walked around the room. "It's queer. I haven't sat in a chair for so long that it feels strange." She pushed at her hair and tried to brush the wrinkles from her skirt. "We must look like savages."

"Come and eat." Mrs. Sinclair set bowls of steaming soup and a platter filled with thick slices of freshly baked bread on the table.

"Butter, too," Elizabeth said wonderingly. "You know, I've dreamed about butter."

While Mrs. Sinclair hurried around, pulling out extra quilts and making up beds for the party, Mr. Sinclair went outside to take care of the horses. John ate three big mouthfuls of soup, then stared at the bowl.

"For some reason I'm not very hungry," he said.

Daniel and Ellen looked blankly at him. "What's the matter with you? This is a feast," Daniel said.

"That's just it." John kept his voice low so Mrs. Sinclair wouldn't hear him. "The soup tastes wonderful, and these people are being so nice to us that I feel terribly guilty."

Daniel had a spoonful of soup halfway to his mouth. He stared at John and put the spoon back in the bowl. "Me, too. All those calves we killed. They must have belonged to the Sinclairs."

Ellen stopped eating and looked first at John and then at Daniel. "What are we going to do? Can we pay for the calves?"

"With what?" John asked. "I haven't a thing in my pockets except a knife."

"Then we had better tell Mr. Sinclair what we did and see what he says. You do it, John." Ellen picked up her spoon, dipped it in the soup, and started eating.

Elizabeth looked thoughtfully at the piece of bread that she had just spread with butter. "That's a good idea. You tell them about it, John."

"No, I can't. You do it, Daniel."

Daniel sighed. "I'm always the goat."

Mr. Sinclair came back into the house. "Your horses

are fine. I rubbed them down and put them into the barn for the night." He broke off and stared at the table. "What's the matter? Aren't any of you hungry?"

Ellen, Elizabeth, and John looked at Daniel.

"Yes, but—" Daniel started off bravely. "But there's something—" He hesitated, gulped, then continued in a husky voice. "Mr. Sinclair, who owns the cattle in the hills to the east?"

Mr. Sinclair smiled. "They must be mine."

Daniel swallowed and cleared his throat. "That's what we thought." He stopped and glanced at John who nodded encouragingly. "Mr. Sinclair, what's a calf about four months old worth?" he asked, almost running the words together.

"Why?"

"Well, I—we killed some calves for food on the way out of the mountains. We would like to pay for them, but there's just one thing: We haven't any money. Do you suppose we can work it off?"

"So that's what's bothering you, and I thought it might be my wife's cooking." Mr. Sinclair laughed and clapped Daniel on the shoulder. "Stop worrying and start eating. People who can get themselves from Missouri to California with wagons can have the calves as a present from me."

Daniel swallowed hard and ducked his head. "I—we—we were awfully hungry," he stammered.

Ellen interrupted. "My brother is trying to say that we are very grateful to you. Every one of us."

"Can you show us the way to Sutter's Fort, Mr. Sinclair?" Elizabeth asked anxiously. "We must get there right away. My husband and brother are up in the mountains with the wagons."

"So's my family," Ellen added, "and there are lots of little children. Even a baby born at Independence Rock in July."

"We'll go the first thing in the morning," Mr. Sinclair promised. "Now you people eat up so my wife can get you to bed."

Elizabeth couldn't sleep. She tossed and turned, thinking about Dr. John and Moses, about Mrs. Murphy whose baby was soon due, about Allen Montgomery and Mary Sullivan, wondering if the company was over the mountains, worrying lest they had been caught in the snow. It seemed that morning would never come.

She was up at the first sign of daylight and hurried to help Mrs. Sinclair fix breakfast. She could hardly eat she was so anxious to start, and smiled gratefully when Mr. Sinclair announced that the horses were ready.

She rode beside him, wishing that her horse had wings. Mr. Sinclair led them across the river and toward Sutter's Fort. Elizabeth sighed when the adobe walls came in sight. "We're finally here. If only we knew that the rest of our company was safe."

"Maybe they are already here, waiting for us inside the fort," Ellen suggested optimistically.

"I'm afraid that's too much to hope for," Elizabeth said. "Let's hurry. We must get a party organized to go back and help them."

ᔖ 15 ᔗ

IN THE mountains the snow was still two feet deep and as sticky as molasses. The oxen floundered and puffed as they pulled the five wagons around the north side of the lake. Captain Stephens and Caleb Greenwood ordered the men to camp and unload the wagons at the base of the mountains jutting up at the western end of the lake.

Mary Sullivan watched Mrs. Martin Murphy, Jr. anxiously as the men stacked supplies on the ground. She had become well acquainted with the young woman during the long journey, and she was concerned for her. She knew that Mrs. Murphy's baby was due soon, and hoped they would reach Sutter's Fort before the child was born.

At sunrise Mary started up the slope carrying an armload of blankets. Her brother John had decided to leave their wagon and had already made packsaddles for the small supply of food, blankets, and clothing they could take with them, so she helped the Murphys with their supplies. She panted in the thin, cold air, trying to fill her lungs. It seemed almost impossible to breathe. After two hours of work, she sat beside Mrs. Murphy watching the men yoke the teams. The oxen leaned forward, straining into the yokes in a desperate attempt to move the empty wagons while the whips cracked above their backs.

About halfway up the thousand-foot slope, the teams stopped. A sheer rock ledge, ten feet high, stretched in front of the oxen, blocking the way.

"What will we do now?" Mary asked her brother. "Oxen can't fly. They'll never get past that ledge." She was so tired that she was close to tears. They had come so far that she couldn't face the thought of failing now, so near California.

"We may have to leave everything except what we can carry, and walk the rest of the way," he answered. "We'll have to use all the horses to pack supplies."

"John Sullivan! You know we can't do that. The small children couldn't make it. Neither can Mrs. Murphy. Her baby's due any day."

Mary looked around frantically, wondering what to do. She saw old Mr. Martin, staggering under a pack of provisions, stare at the rock wall in despair. The faces of the emigrants were grim as the wind whipped their hair and cut through their clothes. The small children huddled under a pile of blankets halfway up the slope. Mary decided that she must fix some hot food while the party was stopped, and she had started gathering brush for a fire when she heard a shout from Caleb Greenwood.

"There's a rift through here," he yelled. "Come this way!"

Everyone crowded around Mr. Greenwood and inspected the narrow opening.

Martin Murphy shook his head. "You can't get wagons or teams through that! We might as well start walking now."

Captain Stephens studied the rift and the slope above it. "Don't give up so fast," he said. "We can do it. We'll take the oxen through one at a time."

The captain and Caleb Greenwood started to unyoke the teams. The rest of the men pitched in to help. One by one, they led the oxen up through the break in the rocky ledge. They carried the yokes through the gap and put them back on the animals. Once the teams were above the ledge, the men came back down and fastened long lengths of chains to the tongue of the first wagon. Mary watched, scarcely daring to breathe, while the chains were carried through the rift, swung out over the ledge, and hitched to the oxen. Captain Stephens and Martin Murphy junior stayed on top to lead the teams while the men laid their shoulders against the wagon wheels.

"Now!" Captain Stephens shouted.

The men pushed and grunted. Sweat rolled down their faces as they shoved desperately at the wagon. Captain Stephens cracked his whip, the oxen moved forward, and the wagon went straight up over the ledge, bouncing as it landed on the sloping ground above it.

Mary picked up her pile of blankets with a light heart and headed for the break in the cliff. They would make it! She knew they could do it.

The second wagon was pulled over the ledge in the same manner. The women and older children straggled up through the narrow opening carrying food, clothes, and blankets, then going down for another load.

At dusk there were wagons at the top, wagons still at the bottom, and supplies scattered on the slope. It took two days of unceasing labor, with men and women wiping sweat from their foreheads, shaking in the icy wind as they carried blankets, tools, food, and utensils over the snow-covered rocks to the top of the mountains and reloaded the wagons.

They were so exhausted by the end of the third day that they camped for the night just below the summit. Mary started singing as she cooked supper for her brothers. She was cheerful, even though she was so tired from carrying supplies up the mountain that she could hardly move. She was glad that John had decided to abandon their wagon. She realized that he was worried about what they would do in California with only the clothes on their backs and the few possessions they could carry on the horses, but she knew they would work hard, and everything would turn out all right.

Early the next morning the company pulled away from the summit. As she mounted her horse, Mary turned to wave at Moses who was standing beside the dying fire. She wondered why anyone would volunteer to stay behind in this forbidding place. She watched as Moses, Allen, and Joseph started swiftly down the mountainside toward the lake, and wondered when she would see them again.

The air seemed suddenly colder and a chill wind slapped Mary's chapped face. A heavy bank of clouds, gray and ominous, rolled across the sky. She shuddered. The clouds looked as if they were bursting with snow.

The route was still difficult. Captain Stephens led them along the crest of the ridge and then down a long hill that was so steep they had to ease the wagons down with ropes. A day later they reached a small river. Martin Murphy junior told Captain Stephens that they had to stop and make camp.

"We can't. We'll get snowed in for sure," Captain Stephens objected.

"We must stop. My wife can't go any farther."

With a deep sigh, the captain swung down from his horse and halted the wagons. "Get busy piling up fuel!" he shouted. "Snow's coming. I can feel it in my bones."

The horses and oxen were driven inside the small circle formed by the five wagons. Then the men chopped down trees and split them into logs, stacking them close to the wagons. They built a huge fire and huddled close together as wind roared through the river gorge. A few scattered flakes of snow fell, stinging their faces. The wind increased to a howl and suddenly fine snowflakes filled the air with a blanket so thick they could hardly see. The fire sputtered and flared, alternately fanned by the wind and dampened by the snow.

"Put it out!" Captain Stephens yelled above the howl of the wind. "Get inside the wagons, cover yourselves with blankets, and stay close together. You can keep warm that way."

Mary Sullivan sat close to her brother John, in a corner of Mr. Martin's wagon. She shivered and pulled the corner of the blanket over her head. The wind whipped a piece of the canvas top loose. John Sullivan, Mr. Martin, and Captain Stephens rushed to lash it down, but snow sifted in on their blankets before the gap was closed.

Mary wiped the melting flakes from her face, wondering if their horses and oxen would survive the storm. Suddenly she heard someone pounding at the tailgate. Mr. Martin untied the lashings and lifted the flap. Martin junior thrust his snow-covered head and shoulders into the wagon.

"Is Dr. Townsend here?" he shouted. "We need him. My wife's going to have her baby."

"I'm coming." Dr. John's face was grave as he swung out of the wagon followed by Captain Stephens. The captain returned in a few moments, shepherding the four small Murphy children into the wagon.

Mary pulled two of them close to her, wrapping them in blankets. "How is Mrs. Murphy?" she asked.

"Dr. John says she'll have no trouble," the captain answered as he wiped snow from the other boys' heads.

Mary shivered as she cuddled the two boys. They soon fell asleep, one leaning on her shoulder, the other with his head in her lap. Her leg prickled. She straightened it cautiously, trying not to disturb the child.

She thought about Mrs. Murphy. What a dreadful night to be having a baby!

The wind howled, and Mary knew the snow was still falling as flakes sifted into the back of the wagon. The hours dragged, and she thought morning would never come. She leaned her head against her brother's shoulder. She dozed at intervals, jerking awake as the boy on her lap rolled over. She pulled the blanket across his shoulders. "John," she whispered. "Isn't it almost morning?"

"Another hour or so," he said. "The storm's dying out. Try to sleep."

She dozed again. When she woke up light was filtering into the wagon. Captain Stephens went to the back and looked out.

"About four feet deep and lots of drifts," he said. "Do you have a shovel, Martin?"

Mr. Martin nodded and found the shovel. Mary gathered the children around her as the men went outside to clear space for a fire and look after the animals.

The youngest Murphy boy looked as if he was ready to cry. She pulled him into her lap. "We'll be warm soon," she said. "Then I'll fix you a stack of flapjacks for breakfast."

As soon as the fire was going, Mary jumped down from the wagon, glad of a chance to move. She was stiff and cold and she stamped first one foot and then the other, wincing as her legs prickled.

Her brother pulled their pack from beneath the wagon and she mixed flapjacks, using the last of their flour.

As she turned to the fire, she saw Dr. Townsend standing close to it. "How is Mrs. Murphy?" Mary asked anxiously. "Is the baby born? Is it a boy or girl? Are they all right?"

"Slow down. You ask questions as fast as Moses does." Dr. Townsend laughed as Mary blushed. "They are fine. Both the mother and the little girl. Mrs. Murphy says she's going to call the baby Elizabeth and for a middle name use the name of this river, when we find out what it is, so she'll know where she was born."

Mary fed the children and then stared around at the piles of snow. The men worked feverishly trying to make a small clearing. They brushed snow from the tops of the wagons, using branches of trees for brooms, and split more logs, piling the wood close to the fire.

The sky was still filled with dirty gray clouds. Mary shivered, wondering if they could survive another storm.

Captain Stephens called the men together, and they gathered around the fire. Martin Murphy junior smiled broadly as he joined them. "It isn't every man who can say his first daughter was born in a place like this during a terrible storm," he said proudly.

"You're certainly right," Dr. Townsend agreed. "But it poses a problem. Your wife can't go on right now, either on foot or horseback, and a newborn baby couldn't survive exposure to weather like this."

"Our miserable, half-starved oxen can't drag the wagons through this snow," Captain Stephens said positively. "We can't use the wagons now."

Martin Murphy spoke up. "Then we men had better go for help. We can't be far from Sutter's Fort. We should be able to return soon with supplies."

Caleb Greenwood and Captain Stephens nodded.

"What about the women and children?" Martin junior asked. "We can't leave them here in the wagons, and we can't take them all with us."

Dr. Townsend walked over to the nearest wagon and picked up an axe leaning against a wheel. "Let's start right now and build a cabin. We can fix a shelter for the women and children and leave some of the cattle here for them to eat."

"We can do more than that," James Miller said. "I'm staying right here with my wife and children. It seems to me we've done enough splitting up."

"I'm staying right here, too," Martin Murphy junior said in a firm voice. "When we get to Sutter's Fort, we'll all get there together."

"We can't all stay," Captain Stephens objected. "Food's too short. Someone has to go for help."

James Miller nodded. "You're right, but I'm staying here with my family."

"I'm staying, too," Mr. Martin said. "I won't leave my daughter. Besides that, I would slow you down."

Captain Stephens walked over to Dr. Townsend and held out his hand for the axe. "That settles it. James Miller and Mr. Martin can handle things here. We'll need to build two cabins, and we had better butcher most of the cows so there'll be enough food."

They worked hard for the next week. The men chopped down trees, trimmed off the branches, and constructed two rude cabins roofed over with rawhides supported by poles. They butchered and hung the meat, hoping that the cold weather would keep it from spoiling.

Early in December the men left for Sutter's Fort, assuring the people remaining on the river that they would soon be back.

Mary Sullivan rode beside John who had refused to leave her behind. "Our family's too small now to be separated," he had said. "I'm not letting you out of my sight."

Mary was glad John felt that way. With the original party split into three groups, she wondered if they would ever find one another. Dr. Townsend looked years older each day. She knew he was worried about his wife and about Moses. As she thought of Moses, she realized that the snow must be much deeper at the lake high in the mountains than it was here. With a sharp pang she wondered if Moses and his companions had survived the storm.

Martin Murphy herded the few remaining cattle, including their two oxen, at her right. He had left the women unwillingly, only because Captain Stephens had reminded him that the food would last longer if fewer men remained in the camp.

They struggled on, wading through deep snow at first, down the valley toward Sutter's Fort. Mr. Murphy constantly urged them to move faster, reminding anyone who complained about the pace or lagged behind of the women and children back at the river who would starve if supplies didn't arrive soon.

The trees thinned out as the steep hills softened to gentle rolling ground. Great oaks dotted the green valley. The countryside resembled that of a midwestern spring because the rain had made the grass sprout. Mary rode at the head of the party beside her brother and Caleb Greenwood. She stared ahead, looking so intently for the fort that her eyes ached as if they were filled with the alkali dust of the terrible desert. Her heart skipped a beat, then lifted like a hummingbird, when she saw a low adobe wall in the distance.

"It's the fort! It must be! Did you ever see any place that looked so beautiful?" Mary shouted and grabbed her brother's arm.

"It looks like a pretty rude fort to me," John Sullivan said, "but yes, I guess you can call it beautiful."

He shielded his eyes from the sun and stared ahead at the gate. "There seem to be a lot of soldiers around. I wonder why." He smiled at Mary. "I'm going to find a place for you to sleep, and then I'll see about selling our oxen. We need supplies."

"This is an impressive place," Mary said as they approached the massive gate of the fort. She glanced curiously at the Indians busy inside the enclosure and stared at the tower where she had seen the barrel of a cannon. The valley seemed so peaceful. She wondered why Mr. Sutter had mounted cannons to guard his fort.

She slid from the saddle and held on to the stirrup, so tired she didn't want to move, while her brother hurried off to see John Sutter.

Mary was directed to a room inside the large, rectangular fort where she was glad to pull off her worn-out shoes and ragged stockings and curl up on a real bed. Just as she was drifting off to sleep, John burst through the door.

"We're conscripted!" John's fists were clenched. His face worked with anger.

"What do you mean, conscripted?"

"Just that! We're in the army. All of the men. Sutter's raising an army for a war. We're all in it."

"What war?" Mary was puzzled. "This is a Spanish country. No one's at war."

"Sutter says there's been a rebellion in the south against Governor Micheltorena, and he has to raise an army to assist the governor. He's appointed Dr. Townsend surgeon and ordered the rest of us into the ranks."

"But what about the women and children back at the river—Mrs. Murphy and her new baby? They need help." Mary's eyes filled with tears.

"That's just it. Sutter won't let us go back for them. He says they'll be all right, and that they are better off in the mountains than down here in the valley where there might be fighting. He says we can go back when the war's over."

Tears streamed down Mary's cheeks. She jumped up and grabbed John's arms, shaking him. "They'll all be dead, John! They'll starve to death!"

⚮ 16 ⚯

Moses stood beside the fire as Captain Stephens ordered the wagons to start away from the summit. All of the gaunt oxen were in use—four yokes to a wagon—as the company moved along the ridge. Moses saw Mary Sullivan, riding beside her brother, fling up a hand and wave. He waved back at her and kicked at the dying embers of the fire, shivering as the wind, whipping across the peaks, tore viciously at his jacket.

The five wagons moved slowly forward as the almost-starved oxen pushed at the yokes. Moses saw Dr. John astride the brown mare, walking the horse behind the last wagon. He turned briskly to Allen, not wanting to show the surge of emotion he felt as he wached his brother-in-law ride away.

"Hadn't we better get started?" he asked gruffly.

Allen nodded. "It's about fifteen miles back to the wagons."

They headed down the slope, sliding, scrambling, working their way around boulders until they reached level ground. They retraced their steps around the north side of the lake, and late in the afternoon sighted the wagons through the trees. Moses leaned against a wheel while Joseph started a fire.

"Let's eat. Then we had better start working on the cabin," Allen said.

Moses groaned. "You never think of anything but work. I'm so tired from scrambling up and down that mountain I could sleep for a week."

Allen pulled an axe from his wagon. "We have an hour of daylight left. Come on."

He swung at the nearest pine sapling. After several strokes of the axe, it hit the ground. Allen trimmed the branches and started chopping at the next tree. Joseph yoked the two skinny cows and hauled the logs to the cabin site they had selected.

With a weary sigh, Moses began to notch the logs. They worked until it was too dark to see, and started in again at daybreak after a skimpy breakfast, putting the back wall of the cabin against a huge boulder for protection from the piercing wind.

"What about a window?" Joseph suggested as they lifted the logs into place.

"Make another hole for the wind to blow through?" Allen asked derisively. "We don't need one. Just leave a hole for the door. We can cover that with a blanket."

"Shall we chink the walls?"

"I don't see why. You've done a good job of notching the logs. They're tight. Let's get the roof on before it starts snowing again. I don't like the looks of the sky," Joseph said.

"We have some hides in our wagon. How about using them?" Moses went for the hides without waiting for an answer.

Moses and Allen worked on the roof the next day, covering it with hides and pine brush while Joseph built a log chimney ten feet high on the outside of the cabin. He used large stones to face the chimney and built a hearth. They were tired but cheerful as they inspected the twelve-by-fourteen-foot cabin.

"It's no beauty, but we should be snug inside it," Allen observed, and whistled blithely as they carried blankets, feather beds, and cooking utensils from the wagons to the cabin. Joseph smiled happily as he built a fire. His grin broadened when the flames leaped up, and the smoke drifted up the chimney.

"It's a good thing we hurried," Moses said as he carried three big pine knots inside and stacked them in a corner. "It's snowing as if it were never going to stop."

"We should do something about the cows," Allen said. "The poor critters are almost starved by now, and the new snow will cover up the few patches of grass that are left."

"We had better butcher them. We can preserve the meat by hanging it on the north side of the cabin. It'll freeze there," Joseph suggested.

"We'll do that early in the morning," Moses said, and they all agreed.

Supper was a scanty meal. Joseph added water to strips of dried buffalo meat and heated it in an iron kettle over the fire.

"This mixture would be more filling if I had some bread to mop up the gravy," Allen said, scraping the last of the buffalo stew out of the kettle.

After supper they banked the fire and went to bed. They were somewhat worried by the howling wind, realizing that the storm was increasing, but they were tired and the cabin was pleasantly warm, so they fell asleep almost immediately.

The storm continued for a week. The wind hammered the cabin and tore at the roof. Moses felt as if his bones were turning to ice. He huddled close to the fire and watched snow sifting through the cracks in the log walls. He toasted his front and froze his back, then turned to reverse the process.

Each morning the snow was deeper, and soon the cabin was almost covered. The supply of buffalo meat was gone, and they had to fight their way around the building to get to the beef they had butchered and hung outside.

"It's a good thing there's plenty of wood close by," Moses said, carrying an armload of logs through the door. "We would freeze for sure if we had to hunt for fuel."

"Fuel's one thing, but game's another." Joseph stamped restlessly around the small cabin. "We need meat, but it's impossible to hunt in this snow. It's so deep that you sink to your shoulders three steps outside the door."

"I'm afraid we're going to starve if we stay here," Allen said. "I never thought the snow would be anything like this."

"The beef's going fast," Moses announced. "With three of us eating, it won't last long."

Allen threw another log on the fire. He walked to the door, pulled the hide covering aside, and peered out at the snow. "I wish we had snowshoes," he said. "Then maybe we could find some game or, if things get worse, we could try getting over the mountains."

"We could make some," Joseph suggested.

"With what? How?" Moses asked.

"How about the wagon bows? They're made of good hickory. We can fill them in with rawhide," Joseph said.

They struggled through the drifts to the nearest wagon, took off a bow, and dragged it back to the cabin. Allen and Joseph cut and bent it into oval shapes to form the hoops while Moses slashed the hides into strips. Joseph took the strips and filled the hoops with a network of rawhide. It was tedious work, but they kept at it without a stop. The snowshoes were their only chance.

Joseph held up a pair of finished snowshoes, and examined them critically. "They don't look too good, but this is the best I can do," he said. "Let's get outside and try them."

Moses had never been on snowshoes before. He was somewhat skeptical as he fastened them, toe and heel, and stepped out into the snow. "They work!" he shouted gleefully as he scooted along on top of the snow. "Let's go hunting."

He headed south from the cabin and made a wide circle. There must be birds or rabbits, he thought, searching under the trees for tracks. Nothing had disturbed the smooth surface of the snow. He trudged slowly back toward the cabin, wondering what could have happened to all the animals. His legs ached, and he varied his gait trying to learn how to handle the snowshoes.

"Come over here," Allen called from the lake shore. "Tracks!"

"They look like fox or coyote tracks to me," Joseph said. "We can't eat either one."

"I don't know about that," Allen answered. "I'm so hungry I would sample most anything."

They returned to the cabin, and Moses prepared the noon meal. "We've eaten a quarter of the meat already," he announced in a worried voice.

Allen rubbed his chin and stared down at the plate he had scraped clean. "We had better try to get out of here before we starve. We can't depend on shooting game. The animals must have gone down below the snow line."

"You're right," Joseph said. "If we wait much longer, we'll be too weak to climb the mountains. We can dry the meat and carry it with us." With that he went outside and came back carrying the frozen beef.

"Is that all of it?" Moses asked.

"No, there's another quarter, but I don't think we can carry it." Joseph hung the meat over the fire so it would thaw.

Allen appraised the beef. "That ought to be ample. We'll leave as soon as the meat's ready. No one would expect us to stay here in danger of starving."

After thawing the meat, they sliced it into thin strips and hung it over poles in front of the fireplace. They continued to hunt, but saw no signs of game and, as more snow fell, they became more and more alarmed.

Two days later they started away from the cabin, using the snowshoes to stay on top of the fluffy snow. Each one of them carried about ten pounds of meat, two blankets, a rifle, and ammunition.

Before they had covered half a mile, Moses discovered that his snowshoes were picking up snow. They became heavy and difficult to lift as the snow crumpled in on top of the shoes with each step. He stopped to remove the caked snow, but a few yards later the snow crumpled in again, weighing down the shoes.

"These things weigh a ton," he panted. "I'm tired."

"So am I," Allen answered with a weary grin. "We'll just have to push on. There's no choice, but we'll make it, Moses."

They skirted the north side of the lake, following the shore line, and then started the thousand-foot climb to the summit.

By the middle of the afternoon, Moses realized, with such a sudden sharp feeling of despair he almost cried out, that he wasn't going to be able to keep up with Allen and Joseph. The backs of his legs cramped with each step as if hot knives were puncturing them. He fell, forced himself back to his feet, staggered a few yards up the slope, and fell again. He rubbed snow over his sweaty forehead and pushed himself up grimly. He clawed and floundered his way through the rocks and drifts, falling, staggering, biting his lips as pains lanced through his legs.

By nightfall he was about fifty yards behind Joseph and Allen who had reached the summit. He had fallen more times than he could count and could stagger forward only a few yards without stopping to rest. His legs cramped, his stomach cramped, and pains shot through his chest as he gasped for breath. He rested for a few moments, then slowly, barely able to walk, pushed on to join his companions.

Joseph chopped down a tree and built a fire on top of the snow while Allen cut piles of branches on which they spread their blankets. They sat beside the fire and ate some of the dried meat, then curled up close together, pulling the blankets around their heads.

Moses lay awake, listening to the soft swish of the snow sliding off the pines. His muscles ached, and his legs twitched. He turned and twisted, but couldn't find a comfortable position. He was so cold that he had to clench his teeth to keep them from chattering. He dozed briefly, then jerked awake as pain shot through his cramped muscles. He thought at least three nights had passed before the sky paled and grew light.

Turning to look at the fire, Moses discovered that it had melted the snow and sunk to the ground, making a circle about fifteen feet wide and fifteen feet deep. It was still burning, but they couldn't get down to it. Moses sat morosely on his blankets, rubbing the calves of his legs.

He munched a small piece of dried beef, wondering if he could manage to stand. Looking ahead at the snow-covered mountain ridges, he realized that many miles of difficult walking faced him. He knew that if he kept going west, he would continue to stagger and fall. Finally he would be unable to get to his feet, and Joseph and Allen would try to help him. One or the other would have to pull him along, then resort to carrying him. They would exhaust themselves, and they would all perish.

"Come, Moses," Allen said. "We must move on."

Moses stared up at Allen for a long moment. Then he made a sudden decision. "I'm going back to the cabin," he said slowly. "You two go on."

"You can't do that! You'll starve. Come on, now. We'll make it." Allen's voice was cheerful and encouraging.

"No, you won't. Not with me along. I'm going back while I can still get there."

"You can't do that," Allen protested. "We won't let you."

Joseph shook his head. "We can't leave you here."

"There's nothing else to do, and you know it. If I go on, we'll all die because you'll try to carry me."

"I know you're right," Allen said, slowly, reluctantly. "But I—I just can't—"

"You can send help back. We'll all have a better chance that way, so don't argue with me. Get started," Moses said firmly. "My mind's made up. I'm going back to the cabin."

↵ 17 ↝

Moses rubbed his sore leg muscles, then pulled himself to his feet, and rolled up his blankets. He winced
and set his teeth as fierce pains stabbed through his
legs. He took a tentative step, almost doubling over,
and turned away so that Allen wouldn't realize that the
pain was agonizing.

He watched Joseph and Allen pick up their packs
and rifles. He felt a terrible loneliness as they started
along the ridge following the route the wagons had
taken a few weeks earlier. He bit his lips, fighting the
temptation to call them back as they vanished behind
the first trees. First Elizabeth, then Dr. John had ridden away. Now Allen and Joseph had disappeared
from sight. He stared at the immense snow-covered
ridges, the tiny lake a thousand feet below, and felt
like the smallest creature on earth. He was completely
alone. Would he ever see a human being again?

He picked up his rifle and pack and forced himself to move. He knew his only chance was to get back to the cabin. He didn't know how he was going to manage it; the fifteen miles seemed an impossible distance to cover, but he had to do it or die.

A frozen crust covered the snow, and Moses discovered he could walk without snowshoes. He went down the slope, sliding, crawling, and staggering, falling against the rocks, dropping his rifle and pack time after time, setting his teeth as he forced himself to get up, to take one step, then another.

When he reached the bottom of the slope, he paused for a few minutes, then started around the edge of the lake, again forcing himself to move his right leg, left leg, then right leg, realizing that if he dropped down to rest he wouldn't be able to get back on his feet. It was a nightmare of falling, grabbing at branches of trees, pulling himself to his feet, staggering, falling again as he followed the shore of the lake. Finally, when he thought he couldn't move another foot, he saw the roof of the cabin through the trees. He set his teeth and pulled himself forward, using the branches of the trees to help him. He fell against the side of the cabin, exhausted and panting. His legs were so cramped that he couldn't step over the nine-inch doorsill. He bent and lifted first one foot over, then the other. Nothing could ache like the backs of his legs, he thought, as he threw wood on the fire, and lit it. He sat on the hearth, stretching his hands out to the flames, then curled up in his blankets and went to sleep, too exhausted to think about eating.

He woke early the following morning, cold and stiff. The hearth was covered with dead ashes. He flexed his numb fingers and gingerly straightened and bent his legs, realizing that he must build up the fire immediately. The calf of his right leg knotted when he tried to stand. He sank down on the blankets and rubbed his legs. His head fell forward, his drowsiness alarmed him, and he realized that he must stand and move, that he must get the fire started.

Once the pine knots were blazing on the hearth and feeling had returned to his numb hands and feet, he discovered he was hungry. What he wouldn't give for some side pork and corn cakes, topped with molasses! Even a chunk of the tough old buffalo he had shot back on the Platte would be welcome. Maybe there was some food left in the wagons that had been overlooked. He knew it was a forlorn hope, but he decided to search carefully. Once he was outside the cabin, he found that the pain in his legs lessened with each step. He waded through the drifts to Dr. John's wagon and pulled himself through the rear opening.

He saw some books that Dr. John had left behind, among them Lord Chesterfield's *Letters to His Son* and a volume of Byron's poems, and carried them back to the cabin. He continued searching through the other wagons and discovered some steel traps in Captain Stephens' wagon.

The traps might work, he thought excitedly. He and Allen and Joseph had seen fox tracks on the lake shore. Perhaps he could trap one, but what could he use for bait? He couldn't use the remaining meat. That scrawny quarter of beef hanging outside the cabin was his last hope, and he didn't have much of the dried beef left because he had given part of his share to Allen and Joseph when they had parted. Then he saw the cows' heads tossed beside the cabin door. He decided they would make adequate bait, so he cut them into pieces and set the traps.

Moses went into the cabin in better spirits. His legs didn't hurt quite so much, and he forced himself to believe his traps would work. He slept part of the afternoon and then fixed a soupy mixture for supper, using the remainder of the dried meat. He was still hungry when he finished, but he didn't dare touch the quarter of beef. He built up the fire and rolled himself in the blankets, hoping he would find something in his traps.

At daybreak Moses scrambled outside to inspect the traps, so anxious to get to them that he ignored the stiffness and soreness in his legs. He was eager to see if he had caught any animals, but was almost afraid to look. He had never been so hungry, and he knew that if he found the traps empty, he would be forced to start eating the last of the beef. Dismayed, he stared down at the body of a dead coyote lying in the first trap, pulled it free, and continued on his rounds. None of the other traps had been disturbed. He hurried back to the cabin with the carcass. It didn't look like much in the way of food. The coyote was mighty scrawny, almost starved, he thought, but he skinned and cleaned it, saving the entrails to use as bait. He put it in a Dutch oven to roast, wondering how long it would take to cook the meat. He was so hungry he could hardly wait. His mouth watered as he watched the pan.

As soon as the meat was done, Moses cut off a chunk and put it in his mouth. He started to chew, and shuddered. It tasted like mud from a swamp, and he spit it out. He tried another bite and forced himself to chew and swallow it, gagging as the meat slid down his throat. As he chewed on the third piece his stomach knotted, and he retched. But it is food, he told himself despairingly. You must eat it or you'll starve.

Maybe boiling would help, he thought with sudden hope. He filled the kettle with snow and set it on the fire to melt. Then he dropped the pieces of coyote into the water and stewed it for two hours. When he lifted the meat out of the kettle and tried again to eat it, it tasted just as bad. It's revolting, he thought, like eating a snake, but it is food, and I'll get it down somehow.

Moses ate coyote for the next three days, trying it broiled over the open fire, stewed, and roasted. No matter what he did, the unpleasant flavor remained. He gagged at each swallow, but he forced himself to eat the meat because he found nothing more in his traps.

The third evening he found two foxes in traps he had set under fallen logs. He was jubilant as he returned to the cabin. Although the foxes were also small and scrawny, he was certain they would be more palatable than coyote.

He put the body of one fox on a spit and sat in front of the fire waiting for it to roast. The smell of the meat was tantalizing. Suddenly he couldn't wait a second longer. He pulled the charred, half-raw meat from the spit, sliced off a piece with his knife, and stuffed it into his mouth.

It was good! As good as hump ribs or a Christmas goose, he thought happily, tearing the meat from the bones with his teeth. He ate half a fox that day and hung the other one outside to freeze.

"If I can keep on catching foxes, I might stay alive," he said aloud, carefully rationing himself so that one fox lasted two days, although he was so hungry that he could have eaten half a fox at each meal.

He inspected the traps morning and evening, usually finding one fox every other day, and occasionally a coyote which he hung on the north side of the cabin, hoping he wouldn't be forced to eat it.

He always carried his loaded rifle with him, ready to shoot if he saw larger game.

One morning a week later Moses saw a crow flying over the cabin. He aimed carefully, fired, and raced forward when the crow tumbled to the ground. He plucked it and took it back to the cabin, putting it in the Dutch oven. Maybe crow would taste good, he hoped, as he waited for it to cook.

"Aargh," Moses said, spitting out the first mouthful. "Crow is worse than coyote."

By this time it was close to Christmas and he was talking to himself. "I might not be so lonely if I hear my own voice," he said, staring through the doorway at the immense expanse of snow. With a sigh he swung the hide covering shut and turned back to the fire.

He thought about the way Elizabeth had celebrated Christmas. In Ohio they had sung carols and exchanged gifts, and in Missouri, too. Last year Elizabeth had knitted him a muffler. She had always hummed carols as she scrubbed and baked, preparing for the holiday. The dinner table had been festive with dried flowers and leaves in the center, and set with Elizabeth's best china. The meal was always climaxed with hot pie brimming with mincemeat that Elizabeth had spent hours making. After dinner Dr. John always read aloud the Christmas story ending with the Wise Men presenting their gifts to the Babe.

Suddenly, desperately, he wanted to celebrate Christmas. He hurried out to the wagon and dug through the trunk until he found the muffler. He carried it back to the cabin and laid it carefully atop the pile of blankets. He sat in front of his fire that evening so lonely he could hardly stand it. Finally he walked over to his bed, glanced at the muffler, pulled the blankets around him, and fell asleep.

He had kept track of the days, and he was certain when he awakened that this was Christmas morning. Moses wrapped the muffler around his neck and pulled on his jacket. He built up the fire, ate a small portion of fox for breakfast, and went outside to make the rounds of his traps. He returned with a fox and a coyote.

He hung the coyote outside the cabin and roasted the whole fox. This was one day when he would have a good meal, a real Christmas dinner. He had saved the small supply of coffee—enough for one cup—that Dr. John had left with him. He decided that this was the day to use it.

He started to eat the fox and found himself unable to finish all the meat. He set it aside and carefully brewed the coffee. Sitting beside the fire, his legs stretched toward the hearth, Moses sipped the coffee slowly, savoring each swallow.

"Merry Christmas, Elizabeth. Merry Christmas, Dr. John," he said softly.

Two weeks later he had trapped eight coyotes. He butchered them and added them to the line outside the cabin. If the supply of foxes ran out, he would have to force himself to eat coyote. His stomach rebelled at the thought, but he told himself sternly that coyotes were edible animals. If he had to eat them, he would.

He continued to make the rounds of his traps every day, although the effort tired him. Toward the end of January he found a fox in the nearest trap. As he approached the second trap, he saw that a fox was caught there too, held fast by a front foot. The fox snarled as Moses came closer, then snapped at his own foot, biting through the bone.

Moses stared for a moment as the fox ran on three legs toward a creek, then he followed quickly, determined not to let the animal escape.

The fox swam the creek and scampered up the opposite bank. Moses raised his gun and fired. He missed! He reloaded quickly and took careful aim at the running animal. This time the fox tumbled over and lay still on top of the snow.

"Hurrah!" Moses shouted. He ran forward and plunged into the water. It was icy cold, so cold he thought it would freeze the marrow of his bones. He waded through the knee-deep creek, then pushed through drifted snow that was chest-high. He grabbed the dead fox and hurried back to the cabin, so cold and wet that he huddled for an hour close to the fire. But he felt triumphant. He had food for another four days!

As the weeks passed, the days ran together, and Moses lost track of time. He read aloud from Dr. John's books by the light of pine knots at night. He skipped Byron's "Elegy" and the poem that started:

> When we two parted
> In silence and tears,
> Half broken-hearted
> To sever for years . . .

Wishing that Byron had been more cheerful, he memorized "She Walks in Beauty." To him the line "But tell of days in goodness spent" described Elizabeth perfectly.

He talked to himself, wondering whether he had been foolish to volunteer to guard the wagons. But he knew he would do it again. It had been a chance to repay Elizabeth and Dr. John for their kindness to him, and to show the men that he wasn't just a stupid

child who could only play tricks or try to shoot thieving
Indians and endanger the entire company.

He remembered wryly the many times Dr. John had
told him it was time he acted like a man. He didn't
feel much like a man. Right now he felt as he had
when he was six years old and Elizabeth had put her
arms around him. Even as he thought it, he realized
that the past months had changed him, that he could
take care of himself now, and if Elizabeth ever needed
help, he could take care of her, too.

He sat in front of the fire, thinking of Elizabeth and
Dr. John, wondering whether they were all right, wishing he could see them. He forced his thoughts away
from his family, knowing that the more he thought
about them, the lonelier he would become.

Then into his mind flashed visions of food. All he
wanted was enough to eat. He could almost see and
smell juicy hunks of buffalo meat, stacks of flapjacks,
topped with molasses, hot corn bread, and crisp side
meat. He wondered if he could stay alive. He hadn't
dared touch the quarter of beef, hungry as he was.
That small amount of meat hanging outside the cabin
was his last hope. If the game gave out completely, he
resolved that he would take the beef and try again to
get over the mountains.

It seemed to Moses that the loneliness was something he could reach out and touch. If only there was

someone to talk with—if only he knew that Elizabeth
and Dr. John were safe. What if Allen and Joseph had
died crossing the mountains? Maybe everyone was
dead. Maybe he would die here, and no one would
ever know what had happened to him.

Moses clenched his fist and hammered it on the
earthen floor. He rubbed his hand across his eyes, swallowed hard, and turned resolutely back to his book.

His head nodded, and he fell asleep. When he awoke
the next morning, cramped and stiff, he wished he
knew what day it was. He told himself that he should
have kept better track of the time, but it must be about
the middle of February, perhaps close to the end of the
month. He had been here alone at least two months,
maybe more, he figured as he went out to make his
morning inspection of the traps.

He trudged back to the cabin with the fox he had
trapped, skinned, and roasted it, then divided the meat
into six portions, setting five aside, and ate his scanty
meal. He dragged in pine knots and huddled close to
the fire. The days were so long and so empty. The time
passed so slowly he thought winter would last forever.
Toward sunset he went outside to check the traps
again.

Moses plodded slowly toward the lake, stopping
abruptly as he saw something move near the shore. He
peered through the trees, realizing that a man was

approaching him. It must be an Indian, he thought apprehensively. He raised his gun as the figure came closer. He sighted down the barrel and steadied himself as he aimed, hoping that the Indian wasn't hostile.

"Moses! Hey, Moses!"

Moses stared, jerking his finger away from the trigger. An Indian wouldn't know his name. It must be—it sounded like—it was Dennis Martin!

Dennis ran the last few yards and clapped Moses on the shoulder. "I sure am glad to see you! You're so skinny you wouldn't cast a shadow." He unslung a pack from his back. "Here's meat, cheese, and bread. Let's go inside and eat."

Without a word Moses turned to lead the way to the cabin. After a step he swung around, facing Dennis. "You're real," he said in a husky voice. "I'd almost forgotten what a real human being looks like."

He stumbled into the cabin and sat down on his blankets, watching Dennis unload the pack, so dazed by the sudden end of his solitude that he wanted to shout; but he couldn't because his throat tightened and his eyes filled with tears.

He stared unbelievingly at the bread and cheese and reached out to touch the food. Then he leaped to his feet and grabbed Dennis by the shoulder. "How's my sister? How's Dr. John? Is Mary Sullivan all right? How's—"

"Slow down. Everyone's all right. Elizabeth's at Sutter's Fort. She arrived there about three weeks after leaving the company. When she heard I was coming back, she asked me to find you. We reached Sutter's Fort in December after leaving the Millers and Mrs. Murphy in cabins we built on a river on the other side of the mountains. They call the river the Yuba at Sutter's place."

Dennis stopped to bite into a piece of roast fox Moses handed him. "What's this? It's good," he mumbled with his mouth full.

"Fox."

Dennis stopped eating. "I don't know as I relish fox."

"Try it. It's not bad at all. I can fix some coyote for you, too, but I won't recommend it."

"Have you been eating coyote?"

"I had to at first," Moses explained. "Only thing I had. But fox is better. There are eleven coyotes hanging on the north side of the cabin. I saved them just in case the supply of foxes ran out. Go on. What happened to everyone and why—?"

"After we reached the Yuba, Mrs. Murphy had her baby so we had to camp. Tons of snow seemed to fall that night. We built two cabins and then the men, except Mr. Martin and James Miller, went on to Sutter's Fort. We were going after provisions, but we couldn't get back."

"Why not? You could walk back."

"Sutter conscripted us," Dennis explained. "He was raising an army to assist the governor and he made us all join. He appointed Dr. Townsend surgeon of the corps. He said the women would be better off in the mountains than down where there might be fighting, and he made us go with the army."

Dennis reached for another piece of fox. "This is pretty good."

"Go on," Moses urged impatiently. "What happened then?"

"We all argued with Sutter. Finally, when we reached Santa Barbara, way down in the south of California, he let us go. So we started right back for the fort and then the Yuba. He gave us supplies for the women."

"Then everyone is all right?" Moses asked the question he hadn't dared ask before.

"Yes, but the women and children had a rough time. The food was about gone when we reached them. They were living on boiled rawhides."

Moses shuddered. "That sounds worse than coyote."

Dennis and Moses left the cabin the next morning after Moses had shown Dennis the line of frozen coyotes. Before they started out, Dennis had taught Moses how to fasten his snowshoes properly so that he could walk without difficulty. They reached the camp on the Yuba River two days later and found the whole group packing up to leave on horseback. There weren't enough saddles to go around so Moses and Dennis rode bareback. Everyone was thin and tired, but they all smiled as they mounted the horses and started toward the valley.

"Just a few days, and we'll be there," Moses said. He called ahead to old Mr. Martin. "Is it still February? What day is it, anyway?"

"It's the first of March," Mr. Martin shouted back. "I figured it out this morning."

Moses was silent, thinking of the long journey they had made and all that had happened to them. He remembered the near disaster with the cattle on the Missouri River, the fear he had felt when they hid from the Sioux, the worn look on Elizabeth's face during the crossing of the desert, and the starving oxen bawling as the stones cut into their feet during the struggle up the Truckee River.

The journey had very nearly ended in the snows of the great mountains, so near and yet so far from the warm California valleys they had dreamed of. Looking back, it seemed as if they had undertaken an impossible task. Yet within a few days he would be with his family, and the hardships would become another epic tale to be told around campfires, like the ones their grizzled guide had told them of his days with the Crows.

"A whole year," Moses said, rousing from his thoughts. "It's a whole year exactly since we left Missouri, and in a few more days we'll reach Sutter's Fort. Then we can start our lives in California."

ᓄᓀ BIBLIOGRAPHY ᔕᔕ

Altrocchi, Julia. Cooley. *The Old California Trail.* Caldwell,
    Idaho: Caxton Printers, Ltd., 1945.

Bancroft, Hubert Howe. *History of California.* Vol. IV. San
    Francisco: A. L. Bancroft & Co., 1886.

Bidwell, John. *Echoes of the Past.* New York: Citadel Press,
    1962.

Billington, Ray Allen. *The Far West Frontier, 1830–1860.* New
    York: Harper & Bros., 1956.

Bryant, Edwin. *Rocky Mountain Adventures.* New York:
    Worthington Company, 1888.

Camp, Charles L., Editor. *James Clyman, Frontiersman.* Port-
    land: Champoeg Press, 1960.

Child, Andrew. *Overland Route to California.* Los Angeles:
    N. A. Kooach, 1946.

Cleland, Robert Glass. *California Pageant, The Story of Four
    Centuries.* New York: Alfred A. Knopf, 1946.

Coy, Owen Cochran. *The Great Trek.* Los Angeles: Powell
    Publishing Company, 1931.

DeVoto, Bernard. *Across the Wide Missouri.* Boston: Hough-
    ton Mifflin Company, 1947.

Federal Writers' Project. *California—A Guide to the Golden
    State.* New York: Hastings House, 1954.

Gray, A. A. *History of California from 1541.* New York: D. C.
    Heath & Co., 1934.

Gregg, J. R. *A History of the Oregon Trail, Santa Fe Trail, and Other Trails*. Portland: Bineford and Mort, 1955.

Hall, Frederick. *History of San Jose*. San Francisco: A. L. Bancroft & Co., 1871.

Hinkle, George and Bliss. *Sierra-Nevada Lakes*. Indianapolis: The Bobbs-Merrill Co., 1949.

History of Marin County, California. San Francisco: Alley, Bowen and Co., 1880.

History of Santa Clara County, California. San Francisco: Alley, Bowen and Co., 1881.

Hoover, Mildred Brooke and Rensch, H. E. and E. G. *Historic Spots in California*. Stanford, California: Stanford University Press, 1948.

Hunt, Rockwell D. *California Firsts*. San Francisco: Fearon Publishers, 1957.

Johansen, Margaret Alison. *From Sea to Shining Sea*. New York: Ives Washburn, 1960.

Keller, George. *A Trip Across the Plains and Life in California*. Oakland: Biobooks, 1955.

Kelly, Charles. *Old Greenwood*. Salt Lake City: Privately Printed, 1936.

Kloppholz, Lowell. *Gold! Gold!* New York: Robert M. McBride Co., 1959.

Lee, W. Storrs. *The Sierra*. New York: G. P. Putnam's Sons, 1962.

Lewis, Oscar. *High Sierra Country*. New York: Duell, Sloan, & Pearce, 1955.

————. *The Autobiography of the West*. New York: Henry Holt, & Co., 1958.

Morgan, Dale L. *The Humboldt, Highway of the West*. New York: Farrar & Rinehart, 1943.

O'Brien, Robert. *California Called Them*. New York: McGraw-Hill, 1951.

Paden, Irene D. *The Wake of the Prairie Schooner*. New York: The Macmillan Co., 1943.

Pen Pictures from the Garden of the World or Santa Clara County, California. H. S. Foote, Editor. Chicago: The Lewis Publishing Company, 1888.

Potter, David Morris, Editor. *Trail to California. The Overland Journal of Vincent Geiger and Wakeman Bryarly.* New Haven: Yale University Press, 1945.

Quigley, Dr. Hugh. *The Irish Race in California and on the Pacific.* San Francisco: A. Roman & Co., 1878.

San Jose Mercury-News. San Jose, California: Dec. 30, 1962.

Stewart, George R. *The California Trail.* New York: McGraw-Hill, 1962.

Stone, Irving. *Men To Match My Mountains.* Garden City: Doubleday, 1956.

Sunnyvale Daily Standard. Sunnyvale, California: Dec. 26, 1962.

Sunnyvale Daily Standard. Sunnyvale, California: Dec. 31, 1962.

Swasey, W. F. *The Early Days and Men of California.* Oakland: Pacific Press, 1891.

Tunis, Edwin. *Frontier Living.* Cleveland: The World Publishing Company, 1961.

Victor, Francis Fuller. *The River of the West.* Hartford: R. W. Bliss, 1870.

Waldo, Edna La Moore. *From Travois to Iron Trail.* New York: Bernard Ackerman, Inc., 1944.

DATE DUE

JUN 28 '84			
APR 0 7 '90			
AUG 2 0 '9			
MAY 17 '96			
APR 21 '98			
GAYLORD			PRINTED IN U.S.A